Death by Misadventure
A Sherlock Holmes Novella

Steve Leadley

A Beach Reeds Publication

Illustrations by Pamela Fine.   For more of Mrs. Fine's artwork
please visit: **www.artbypamfine.com**

A Beach Reeds publication

Library of Congress Cataloging-in-Publication Data
Leadley, Steve
Death by Misadventure/Steve Leadley
Beach Reeds, 2013

Detective Fiction/Mystery Fiction/Historical Fiction/Historical Mystery

ISBN: 978-0-9800944-6-6

Look for other books by Steve Leadley at:
www.steveleadleyauthorpage.weebly.com

Foreword

For those who have not read the other Sherlock Holmes novellas I've penned, my treatment of the great detective is intended to honor the original conception of the characters as they were created by Sir Arthur Conan Doyle as well as mimic Doyle's style to the best of my ability. Some literary agents and publishers expressed doubt that my approach would be viable and urged that I "reinvent" Holmes and Watson in some new and revolutionary way. Suggestions ranged from sending them into outer space, have them time-travelling, or battling supernatural adversaries such as zombies and vampires.

I have no quarrel with those who enjoy alternate versions of Doyle's creations or the twenty-first century television incarnations of Sherlock Holmes; although personally I am not a fan of such efforts. To me, the Victorian Era is the canvas upon which Holmes and Watson are painted and although I enjoy a good mystery whatever the period, I have no interest in removing Doyle's consulting detective and his 'friend and colleague' to an alien timeline or involving them in unrealistic plots.

Although my knowledge and expertise of Holmes does not approach that of a great many Sherlockians, as a reader I am a fan of Doyle's canon. My one complaint is that with fifty-six short stories and four novels, Sir Arthur left me wanting more. I was of the opinion that others likely felt as I did and would welcome traditional Holmes stories that could conceivably fit into the original canon. Given the sales of my other Sherlock Holmes novellas, it appears that I was correct.

Some true historical personages appear in this story; although in a fictional context. I do not want spoil what lies ahead but would like the reader to know that what may seem to be the most improbable facet of this tale may have actually existed. I encourage some online research after reading this story as an illustration of the adage that sometimes "truth is stranger than fiction."

SL

CHAPTER 1

I had seldom been so worried about Sherlock Holmes.

Those familiar with my chronicles may say: "But what of the time he was nearly killed by Baron Gruner's thugs? Or when you believed a rare Asiatic disease had him at death's door? Were you not more distressed when he almost brought about his own departure by purposely inhaling the poison of 'the devil's foot'?"

It is true that I feared for my friend's life on those occasions and in fact dozens of others. However my anxiety in this instance did not stem from a dread of such imminent calamity as in the aforementioned adventures. In fact, my concern was not for my friend's physical well being at all, but rather that of his psyche. Holmes once told me: "I am a brain Watson, the rest of me is mere appendix." At that moment, that brain was languishing in tortured flagellation.

If you have followed my comrade's career you are doubtlessly familiar with his many and varied successes. However, on the day of which I am reflecting, Holmes was seething over what he considered to be one of his most inauspicious defeats.

My friend's services had been engaged by a Norfolk gentleman whose wife had become unhinged over a series of etched stick figures that began appearing on their property. Holmes set to work deciphering the strange hieroglyphics and uncovered the rather nefarious meaning behind these 'dancing men.' Despite our haste to prevent disaster, our arrival in Norfolk was met with the somber news that Holmes's client had been killed, and his wife was clinging to life. Although Holmes succeeded in apprehending the villain responsible, he was now castigating himself for not solving the puzzle sooner and averting the tragedy.

I have at times described Holmes as arrogant and it can never be said that he did not pride himself upon his gifts. However this hubris was double-edged; when he felt that he fell short of his own high standards it cut him more deeply than any physical weapon.

Such were the circumstances this very morning. Holmes was morose beyond consolation and sat in our rooms staring into the empty fireplace, exactly where I had left him when I retired the previous night.

I suspiciously looked about the room, but thankfully saw no signs of the dreaded syringe case. Upon the table lay a plate with an untouched scone and a tranquil cup of coffee. Next to these sat the morning papers which were uncharacteristically undisturbed. I glanced concernedly at the prone, lounging figure across the room and opened my mouth to address him, before thinking better of it. The evening before I had tried to rouse Holmes from his miserable stupor and had been rebuked by a stony silence. I instead took a seat at the table and filled my cup from the coffee pot and removed a piece of quick-bread from the basket.

"Perhaps an item in the paper might stir Holmes," I thought, leafing through the pages. "Oh my," I said aloud. "It appears that an earthquake occurred in Manhattan, bringing police and ambulances to a Houston Street neighborhood. That is singular, is it not?" said I, peering around the page. "Tremors in New York are unheard of as it is and one that is isolated to such a small area is bizarre indeed."

The back of the head that faced me moved slightly, but no response was forthcoming. My concern was suddenly eclipsed by warmth of temperament and I dropped the paper and stalked over to my friend, taking the seat opposite him.

"Holmes, see here," I began in an agitated manner. "You must shake out of it. No man could have done more in that Norfolk affair. In fact, had you not been involved, the guilty party would have escaped completely."

Finally I saw a sign of animation in my flat-mate, as a wry smile flitted across the corner of his mouth. "Watson," he said, turning to me. "Your friendship is indomitable." He winced slightly as he adjusted himself in his chair. "Had I more samples of those messages sooner, I am certain that I would have broken the cipher in time. But that is the rub, friend Watson. I should have insisted that if any new hieroglyphics appeared, a copy be sent immediately by post. Instead, a fortnight went by before our client travelled back here with several of the messages in tow."

3

"But Holmes, the danger only showed itself after you had deciphered the messages you just mentioned. Your logic is circular. You could not have imagined the hazard that existed *until after* you had them in hand to help you unravel the code. And only the final message, which *was* sent by post, alerted you to impending disaster. If you recall, at that point we took the first available train out to North Walsham."

"Perhaps you are right," he replied in a placating, unconvincing tone. "Pray hand me my pipe and tobacco."

This I found as a reassuring gesture and a first sign that my friend's melancholy may be lifting. I gladly retrieved both the clay pipe and Persian slipper of tobacco from the mantle and handed them over. "Holmes," I said, trying to push my advantage. "What say we pay a visit to the Turkish baths?"

"Just the thing, Watson. I think you've hit upon it," he said in a welcoming, if subdued tone. "I shall finish this pipe and dress presently."

Bolstered by the mild, but comforting change in demeanor, I rang downstairs and a moment later Billy, our page, appeared at the door.

"Yes, Dr. Watson?"

"Billy, Mr. Holmes and I will be leaving in a half hour or so. Hail us a hansom in about that time."

"Right, you are, Doctor," said he, tipping his cap.

It did not take long for Holmes to tidy himself and transform from the languid, disheveled brooder into the guise of a respectable Londoner. Billy was efficient as always and a cab was waiting as we stepped out into Baker Street.

"Northumberland Avenue, the Baths!" I ordered the driver as we climbed inside.

It was still early and the morning air was refreshingly crisp for an English summer. Holmes was quiet, but his eyes were brighter and he seemed to grow more alert as the sights and sounds of the ante meridiem busied to prepare the great city for its day.

As we were passing the railway platform I noticed a police wagon and a handful of officers holding back a small crowd of commuters attempting to access the terminal.

"It appears that some trouble has occurred," I said to Holmes, drawing his attention out of my window. "Someone may need medical assistance. Driver," I called, striking the ceiling with my stick, "Pull up by the platform." Holmes remained silent but a gleam flickered in his eye. I paid the cabman and followed Holmes over to the small throng.

"You will just have to wait," a red-faced constable was explaining to an angry man holding a leather satchel.

"I must be in Whitehall by eight!" he bellowed, shaking the handle of his umbrella in the constable's face.

Another man made a similar ruckus about a different destination, threatening to bypass the police. A stout officer, more boisterous then the first met this declaration by stating in no uncertain terms that there was an investigation underway and the lot of them would find themselves removed to the police van if they dared interfere. If his commanding voice and stern facial expression had proved insufficient to convince the group, the removal of his club, which he rhythmically clapped into his other hand, punctuated his seriousness and reduced the assemblage into quiet grumbling.

"Pardon," I called, pushing through the small crowd. "I am a doctor; can I be of any use?"

"Not hardly. Perhaps if you were an undertaker," the heavy officer scoffed.

Just then a plain-clothed man rounded the corner of the police wagon. "Mr. Holmes! I thought that I noticed you!" the tall, fair-haired inspector announced. I immediately recognized the amiable Tobias Gregson. "And Dr. Watson!" he added. "Let them through," he commanded to the uniformed men.

The name of my companion had an immediate effect upon the red-faced policeman whose expression shifted to one of admiration. However the portly constable merely used his girth to push several men aside without a hint of recognition for one who had so advanced the methods of his profession.

"Inspector, how are you?" I asked as we made our way beyond the human barricade.

"Tolerable, Doctor. Tolerable." When we were out of earshot of the small group, he turned to my friend. "Mr. Holmes, I should like to have your opinion on this matter, if you don't mind."

"What seems to be the issue, Inspector?" replied Holmes.

"Well Mr. Holmes, I suspect that it hardly bears your expertise, but as you know I always value your input," Gregson stated as he led us toward the tracks. "It appears that a fellow slipped and fell from the platform and then was struck by a train."

"That is unfortunate," Holmes returned.

"Yes, and I never would have called on you regarding the matter but when you appeared by happenstance..." Gregson broke off as a thought dawned on him. "You are here accidentally, aren't you? Were you upon a scent? Is this incident part of one of your investigations?"

"Ha!" laughed Holmes. "Gregson, you improve every day. No, we were on our way to the Turkish Baths when our good doctor here saw the commotion and thought he might offer some medical aid. I know nothing of this," he said, waving his stick at the scene.

"Yes, yes," Gregson smiled. "Well, as I said, it seems to be a dreadful accident, but as you know, I never shun your counsel and if you have a few moments, I would be grateful of your opinion."

Holmes had often stated that Gregson was the best brain at Scotland Yard and although I suspect that this was mostly due to the inspector's willingness to forego vanity and consult him if it benefitted a case, it warmed Holmes's estimation of the man.

"If Dr. Watson does not object. I know he has his heart set upon the baths," Holmes replied, clapping a hand upon my shoulder.

"Not at all," I added, glad to see my friend returning to his old self, despite the sad cause of his revival.

Gregson led us some little distance away from the platform to the far side of the tracks. There another policeman stood to one side smoking, while a plain-clothed individual huddled over the crumpled heap lying nearby.

As we approached Holmes asked, "So am I to take it that there were no witnesses?"

"Correct. It appears that the man fell from the platform last night and was struck by the express as it passed through. There would be no one on the platform at that time as no train would be stopping."

"Ah, but there *was* someone on the platform," Holmes returned. "Your unfortunate victim. Does it not strike you as odd that he would be waiting for a train where none would stop?"

The inspector shrugged his shoulders. "He had a near empty flask in his pocket and was possibly inebriated; which could explain not only his error in the train schedule, but also his tumble from the platform."

"Is that the spot where he was discovered?" asked Holmes as he pointed ahead.

"Yes, he has not been moved."

As we reached the body, the inspector who was bent over the corpse stood, and before he had even turned around, I recognized the small form of Lestrade, who unlike Gregson, was less enthusiastic about my friend's methods. Lestrade was not above asking for Holmes's assistance, nor always niggardly in his praise, but he was prideful and displayed a decided preference for the tenacious, dogged approach standard in the Yard as opposed to Holmes's more cerebral techniques.

"Mr. Holmes, I think we have this one well in hand," the thin-faced, dark-eyed man stated flatly.

"Undoubtedly," Holmes returned cordially. "We were but passing by and Gregson here asked if we would like to see the body. It is a mere curiosity, Inspector, nothing more." This seemed to mollify Lestrade somewhat, as his demeanor became less defensive.

"Is that the flask?" Holmes asked, pointing to the silver object seated upon the ground nearby.

"Yes," Gregson interjected, retrieving the item.

Holmes twisted off the cap and smelled inside, offering the orifice to my own nose.

"Vodka, I should think," said I.

Holmes nodded his approval. "Splendid, Watson. Not everyone can detect its faint aroma." He turned to Gregson, "No identification on the body?"

"No, nothing upon him but that flask," said Gregson.

9

We moved over to the broken form. The body was badly mangled. His face however was intact. He appeared to be a man approaching the age of thirty. He was slightly built, perhaps five foot seven in height. The man was in possession of a round, well-formed skull flowing with substantial, dark hair albeit receding at the temples. A thick goatee adorned his muzzle, the mustache of which obscured his top lip. His clothing was decidedly working class, but not overly worn.

"Have you examined the inside of his clothing? Are there any identifying marks within?" Holmes asked.

Lestrade responded, "The labels are all common English brands; nothing unique in any way, save the number '63' that is inked upon the interior of this cap," he said as he handed forth the cloth hat.

Holmes and I both peered inside where the numbers were etched. They were a bit odd given the block-like hand in which they had been written, but I thought otherwise uninteresting, although I noticed my friend's eyebrow rise slightly upon his inspection of the head-covering.

Unexpectedly, my companion fell upon the ground and put his face close to that of the dead man's. He peered minutely at his beard and even sniffed at it like some type of human bloodhound. Abruptly he jumped to his feet and turned to Lestrade.

"Thank you," he said, returning the cap he still held in his hand. "I am sure that you gentlemen will handle this with your characteristic resolve. Dr. Watson and I are late for a rendezvous with some steam. I bid you good day," he tipped his bowler to the inspectors and headed back toward the street in order to hail another hansom.

Lestrade offered us a businesslike farewell as we departed but Gregson was at our heels. "Do you think we have judged this rightly, Mr. Holmes?" he asked.

"No Inspector, I do not."

Gregson was taken aback. "What flaws do you see?"

"My dear Inspector, as I said, Dr. Watson and I have an appointment. I suggest that you re-think your conclusion and if you still would like my input, come around Baker Street later this afternoon." Holmes paused before reaching the street. "Oh, can we have a quick look at the platform before we depart?"

"Most certainly," Gregson returned, now anxious to re-examine the spot himself.

We ascended the structure and Holmes walked the length of the terminal, scanning the pavement as he went. Finally he stopped at the end closest to the direction where the body had been found and used his stick to point to two parallel and almost indistinguishable black marks that ran about a meter in length, right to the edge nearest the tracks. "Did you see these?" he asked Gregson.

"I barely see them now," the inspector replied.

"Reflect upon them, Inspector. They are suggestive. Come Watson, let us be off." With that my friend led the way back to the street, leaving Gregson staring intently at the cement.

Holmes and I spent a refreshing morning at the baths. The Turks may be chastised for their treatment of the Armenians or the Sultan's penchant for expanding his empire, but their contribution to relaxation bears commendation. My friend often vacillated between the unhealthy polarization of frenzied activity and dejected idleness. The baths however allowed him to physically unwind without walking along the dangerous precipice brought about by mental stagnation.

As we sat in our favorite upper floor drying room, I could see that Holmes was pensive. He was quiet, but thankfully none of the previous gloom remained.

"Why is it you feel Lestrade and Gregson have missed the mark?" I posed.

"Oh, there are a number of indicators," he said offhandedly. "Ruminate upon the situation yourself, Watson and when Gregson comes round you can see if you or he finishes with the better score," he replied, before slipping once more into the meditative state upon which I dared not further intrude.

"Did you see these?" he asked Gregson.

13

That afternoon we were back in Baker Street and Holmes had almost fully recovered. He had moved to his chemistry bench and was mulling over one of his odorous problems when the bell rang.

"Ah, Watson," said he. "Here is our good inspector. I hope you have reached some conclusions of your own," he chided as he replaced a test tube in its rack.

A sharp knock presently followed. "Mr. Holmes, Inspector Gregson, sir," Billy called from the hallway.

"Show him in, will you, Watson?" he asked as he removed his heavy apron and hung it upon a hook.

"Good afternoon, Inspector. I see you have retrieved your watch from the jeweler. You must take care not to over-wind it in the future," Holmes reprimanded as he took a seat and gestured for Gregson to do the same.

"My watch? Why yes… How did you know?"

"You were without it this morning, and although it was possible (though not likely) that at the time you had forgotten it, I see that it now has a new stem, the repair necessitated by over-winding. Therefore it is logical to assume that it was not upon your person because it was in for repairs and you have since reclaimed it."

"Correct as usual, Mr. Holmes. I had no idea that you had noticed it was not on me this morning."

"If I did not take note of such things, I would be of little service to you upon your present errand," Holmes smiled.

"I suppose that is true," Gregson grinned in return.

"So Inspector, have you altered your opinion at all about this *accident*?" Holmes asked, lighting his pipe.

Gregson shifted in his seat. "I have indeed, Mr. Holmes. When you pointed out those marks, I began to think about their possible cause. Looking back at the victim, it turns out that the heels of his boots are made of India rubber. I believe that they left those marks."

"Capital, Inspector! Watson, had you reached the same conclusion?"

"I did suspect that they were left by the decease's shoes but had not narrowed their origin to the heels in particular."

"Well, we won't favor Gregson too greatly on that one. After all, he had the opportunity to go back and re-examine the fellow after I showed him the marks."

"Watson, we shall give you a try on this point," Holmes continued. "Since the marks are from the man's heels, what does that reveal?"

I thought for a moment. "That he heard the locomotive approaching and ran to catch it. When he realized that the train was not going to stop, he skidded to an abrupt halt but overshot the edge of the platform and fell onto the tracks."

"Do you concur with that account, Inspector?" Holmes queried.

"I am afraid that I do not," returned Gregson. "If events had transpired as Dr. Watson suggests, the location of the body should have been different. It seems that sliding over the edge would put him in contact with the nearer side of the train and thus he should have ended up on the nearer side of the tracks, and I would think closer to the platform."

"Well done, Gregson!" Holmes commended.

"So, if he did not fall from the platform, he... must have been thrown!" I stated as I formulated the only logical possibility.

"Most certainly," said Holmes. "He was grabbed by two men, one on each arm, who after relieving him of his billfold, gave him a running toss in front of the train. The marks are of course from his attempt to put the brakes on his impending demise. He was struck fairly high upon the face of the engine and upon its far quarter. Surely no one man could throw the poor fellow that far. Thus he ended up on the other side of the tracks and that distance down the line."

"Watson," Holmes continued, turning in my direction, "How do we know that the unfortunate chap was robbed?"

"I would think that the lack of a wallet upon him is sufficient, but it also seems absurd that he would ascend a platform without any means of paying for passage on the train."

"You are coming around, Watson!" said Holmes. "He was likely being pursued and hearing a train approaching, ran up to the platform hoping for a means of escape. Obviously he did not know that the train would not stop. The pair caught up with him, wrestled away his billfold and pitched him to his doom."

Holmes turned toward Gregson. "Inspector, have you had any luck indentifying the victim?"

"No, Mr. Holmes. On that score we are still at an impasse."

"I suggest that you focus your inquiry in the East End amongst the Slavic neighborhoods. See if anyone reports a missing man with the initials B.Z."

"The vodka? Is that what leads you to suspect he is Slavic?" I interjected.

"That, the fact that his facial features bear some characteristics of Eastern Europe--did you not note the round head, Watson? I have written a monograph upon the subject that I shall have to retrieve for you-- And also that there were olfactory remnants of borscht in his facial hair."

"And what of the 'B.Z.?'" Gregson asked as he jotted in his notebook.

Holmes laughed. "You have become infected by Lestrade's lack of imagination. The '63' upon the tag are not numerals but letters. They represent 'Be' and 'Ze' in the Cyrillic alphabet."

"So you don't know the man, Mr. Holmes?" Gregson asked, closing his pad.

My friend was somewhat taken aback by the question. "Certainly not, Inspector. What would make you think so?"

Gregson pulled a small piece of paper from his coat pocket and passed it to Holmes. "Upon removing one of his boots, the coroner found this."

My friend looked at the slip without comment and then handed it to me. On it was scrawled: HOLMES 212.

"It seems, Mr. Holmes, that he was going to seek you out but had your address off a bit," the inspector stated.

After Gregson had left, Holmes became pensive. He sat smoking, his brows knitted in thought.

"Do you still believe that the motive was robbery?" I asked, resuming the seat across from my friend.

"What's that? Oh. Impossible to say, Watson. It may have been robbery or perhaps some other dastardly intent. However, premeditation now seems more likely than a random attack."

"So you do think that he had planned to come and consult you."

"Perhaps," replied Holmes. "What intrigues is the location of that note. Why would he secret it away in his shoe? It is certainly not a criminal offense to carry an address in one's pocket." He exhaled a cloud of blue smoke. "If a weapon had been found upon him, I would suspect that he intended some mischief upon me."

"I suppose that for some reason he wanted to keep his visit confidential," I speculated.

"Yes…"

"Do you believe he was killed to prevent him from seeing you?" I queried.

"Hmm. That could be the case, or perhaps it was over the issue he wished to bring to my attention."

Next day, a gentleman arrived, concerned about a stock certificate that had gone missing from his locked study. My friend accepted the assignment and was gone from our rooms before noon.

It was just before teatime when I returned from attending to a hypoglycemic haberdasher in Oxford Street and found Holmes reposed in a padded armchair, puffing away at his pipe. Although several of his indexes lay piled in his lap, his eyes were half-closed. I knew this reflective state well.

"Some notorious felon a suspect in the missing stock case?" asked I, pointing to the indexes as I hung my hat.

"Eh? No, Watson, I cleared that matter up in an hour. I'm afraid that one won't make it into your annals. Mr. Armbruster's fear was as misplaced as the certificate itself, which he had merely inadvertently closed in a book."

"Some new business then?" I furthered, placing my medical bag at home in its cabinet.

19

"Not quite fresh, but not yet stale, either," he quipped. "That business with the train death. There are some points that gnaw at me…"

If further comment was to be made I shall never know as the gentle knock of Mrs. Hudson was followed by the noble woman herself carrying a tray of tea and biscuits.

"I heard you return, Doctor," she said. "I hope that you can abide a bit of respite?"

"It is most welcome," I returned, pulling up a seat at the table.

"And you, Mr. Holmes?" our landlady queried.

Rather than reply, Holmes removed the volumes from his lap and stalked into his bedchamber, closing the door.

"I am sorry, Mrs. Hudson," I apologized for my roommate. "He is obviously lost in thought over some problem."

"Oh, Dr. Watson," she chuckled. "I've learned long ago not to take offense at the eccentricities of Mr. Holmes. He's been living under this roof long enough that I know he means no offense by such actions."

I had nearly finished my tea when a man emerged who little resembled my friend. The person who stepped from his room had a ruddy complexion hid partially by a dark moustache and beard. His hair likewise had turned two shades darker. Small, round spectacles made his eyes appear beady. His dress was much more bedraggled than the usually impeccable attire of my companion, betraying a man of the laboring class.

"So, I take it you are embarking on some incognito work?" I smiled, as I finished off the biscuit in my hand.

"Da, I plan on spending some time in the East End. Do not be alarmed if I do not return in a timely fashion," he stated through a thick Russian accent. He pulled a cloth cap upon his head and gave my shoulder a pat as he passed, before disappearing through the door.

I saw little of Holmes that week, as he came and went at odd hours. Passing glimpses confirmed that he was still upon his hunt in the East End. Mostly he continued as the bespectacled Russian but I also witnessed him leave our rooms as a Hassidic Jew and even as a heavy-set, babushka-wearing woman.

"Ah, Watson," I heard as I stepped from my bedroom one morning. "What would you say to a little adventure this evening?"

Standing across the room stood the dapper consulting detective more familiar to my eye. He was paging through one of his indexes, but replaced it upon the shelf and came over to join me in the breakfast Mrs. Hudson had already delivered upon the table.

"So your foray into the East End has borne fruit?" asked I, taking a seat.

"That is hard to say," he replied, seating himself across from me. "I tried to frequent as many establishments as I could in the Russian quarter, raising benign questions about the ill-fated man. Mostly I was met with idle comments but nothing concrete, not even a name. Fortune shined on me however at one juncture when

21

in a tearoom I overheard two men discussing the tragedy." He paused as he poured himself some coffee. "My Russian is minimal, Watson. I fear the bit I acquired investigating the Trepoff murder in Odessa has retreated to a back corner of my brain. Although I was able to coax those I engaged into conversing in English, when acting as a mere fly on the wall I had to make do, grasping as much as I could when eavesdropping on this pair."

"You overheard something of value, then?"

"Perhaps. They alternated between English and Russian and I was able to piece together that they were discussing the dead man. They called him by name. Well by his Christian name, anyway."

"So they knew him!"

"It appears so. They referred to him as 'Boris.' As best I could make out, he was supposed to meet someone called Stephan, but that meeting never occurred as his demise preceded the event. One of the men said that he himself was to meet this 'Stephan' this evening at The Black Horse, a pub in Aldgate High Street."

"Do you suppose these two were confederates of the dead man-or perchance the ones who killed him?"

"That I cannot say; although if it is the latter, this Stephan is in imminent danger."

"Did you follow either of them from the tearoom?" asked I.

"Ha! Watson, what a grand schemer you are becoming. No, had I been able to alter my appearance, I should have, but I had no lair nearby to change and thought that I would be too recognizable as the man seated next to them in the tearoom. Yet I might have hazarded it, if I had not gained knowledge of this meeting tonight but I did not want to risk arousing suspicion and have the rendezvous aborted."

"So we are to secret ourselves in this pub tonight?"

"So you are game? Good old Watson, as audacious as ever! Yes. We will see what we can see and overhear what we can overhear."

I was still unaware what element in this episode had piqued my friend's curiosity to the degree that prompted him to decide to put it at the forefront of his schedule. Although I may say without doubt that I was Holmes's greatest confidant, he was still by nature one who by and large kept his own counsel until he had anything definite to convey. Certainly the fact that this "Boris" was the victim of murder, rather than accident, was noteworthy. However, Holmes did not seem overly intrigued until his own name had been found upon the dead man. This then seemed the obvious catalyst in drawing him further into the matter though I failed to conjure how it could be singular enough to ensnare my companion's complete attention. By the time of this adventure, Holmes's notoriety was such that anyone with a difficult problem might seek him out.

At half-past eight we were seated in a hansom, headed toward Aldgate. As instructed by Holmes, I was attired in apparel that was less appealing than my normal garb, but far from threadbare either. My friend was similarly clothed, and with his mussed hair and low cap, he hardly looked himself. Apparently The Black Horse was one of those hundreds of establishments above the dingy barrooms meant to accommodate the underbelly of London; yet neither was it a place where a member of the professional class would feel at home.

Holmes had us alight two blocks from our destination. My friend had not asked me to bring along my revolver, so I did not believe that he anticipated a threat to our person, but as we stepped to the street I reconsidered when I witnessed him tuck his loaded riding crop under his coat at the small of his back.

"Now Watson, give me a two minute head start on you. I do not wish it to appear that we are together, at least not at this juncture. We are a good twenty minutes ahead of the scheduled meeting but it is possible that at least one of the participants is already in the pub. Do not situate yourself too near me until I give this sign." He scratched his nose with two fingers. "I will flash it when I identify the man from the tearoom. Then, as inconspicuously as possible, sidle as near as you dare and hopefully we will be able to obtain some information as the two conduct their meeting."

I followed Holmes's instructions and lingered upon the corner for the duration he had indicated before sauntering down Aldgate High Street. In the middle of the second block I saw the painted sign above a doorway bearing no lettering, but the image of a black stallion rearing upon its hind legs provided sufficient identification. The establishment was as imagined; non-descript as watering holes go, interchangeable with so many in the city. A pair of men pushed past me, up the two steps leading into the pub and as the door opened, the unintelligible hum of voices spilled out onto the street, punctuated by the clanking of glassware and the occasional peal of laughter. It was but a moment and I had scurried up the stoop and through the door that had yet to fully close.

"A pint," I ordered of the barkeep as I squeezed between two patrons at the rail.

It was only after I had taken a sip from the warm, although not altogether bad, ale that I furtively scanned the room. The place was small, and busy. Along the left wall sat the bar at which I stood. The opposite wall was lined with booths and the area in between housed a half dozen tables. Behind the tables lay an open area for dancing and beyond that, a small stage upon which a man had just begun banging away on a piano. Three quarters of the persons in the establishment were male, but apparently a number of women also found The Black Horse to their liking as they plied the particular talents of their sex, coaxing drinks from those wearing trousers.

It took me a full five minutes to locate Holmes. He had taken up residence in a corner near the water closet. This maneuver struck me as an appropriate display of my friend's surveillance acumen.

If he had difficulty finding his quarry, his prey would certainly come to him when the effects of libation took their toll.

I had been in the pub a quarter hour and the signal from Holmes had yet to be given. I was growing both impatient and apprehensive, wondering if for some reason the meeting had been cancelled or moved when I witnessed a pair of my companion's thin fingers relieve a fictitious itch upon his snout. He nodded toward a duo of new arrivals at the other end of the bar and began making his way across the room. I returned his signal as a countersign, which I am sure that Holmes caught, and yet he gave the indicator again; in order to leave no doubt, I presumed. I lifted my glass from the ring-stained wooden surface and began picking my way through the crowd in the direction of our targets. One of the men wore a goatee beard, not unlike the dead man. His hair was dark and coarse. He appeared to be in his twenties and his face was pale as if he had spent a great deal of time indoors. His cohort seemed slightly older, perhaps not far over the age of thirty. His hair was lighter and thinning on top. His face was clean-shaven and if my estimations held true, his height reached six foot-three; causing him to tower over his partner by a good six inches. As I snaked my way through the crowd, I wondered if these two seemingly benign fellows were in fact the murderers we sought.

CHAPTER 3

It would be no easy task to position myself close to the pair. They had either fortuitously, or by design, situated themselves around the corner of the bar so that the wall was at their back and only the spot to their left afforded the possibility of access. Luckily the patron who had been standing there ordering a pint received his beverage and vacated the spot. Whether Holmes or I reached the opening first would be determined by how skillfully each navigated the ever-changing obstacles created by the lively crowd. I was but a few feet from my destination when much to my chagrin a dark-haired, thick-mustached chap wearing tinted glasses claimed the place as his own. I was gritting my teeth in frustration when I felt a hand upon my shoulder.

"This way Watson," Holmes whispered in my ear as he retreated a few feet to a place along the wall, not far from where our quarry sat.

"I had almost reached that spot," I hissed from behind the lip of my glass as I brought it up to feign a drink.

Holmes did not reply but quickly drained the remainder of his ale and pushed forward to the bar, squeezing between the wall and the taller, fairer individual. Holmes leaned on the bar, empty glass in hand. To all outward appearances he seemed to be trying to order a refill but he cleverly called for the bartender just as the man

27

turned his back, affording him more time next to the duo. In less than three minutes however, the conscientious barkeep noticed my friend and slid his glass under the tap. The uncomfortable, sideways position Holmes had been forced to assume pinioned against the wall might not rouse suspicion for one attempting to acquire a pint, but once that objective had been achieved, he certainly could not remain there without tipping his hand, thus my friend was soon back at my side.

"Any luck?" I asked in a soft voice surely audible only to Holmes as the din of the pub droned around us.

Holmes clapped a hand upon my shoulder and rocked his head back in mock laughter, employing some of his acting talents. As he pretended to chortle, he grunted, "Hardly, Watson. They were speaking in Russian. Suppose you finish that pint and give a try yourself."

I downed the remaining liquid and wedged my way into the same space Holmes had used. The cacophony of the barroom made it difficult to discern the low voices of the pair next to me. The best I could make out was an occasional word in Russian, confirming that as when Holmes attempted his eavesdrop, they were still conversing in that Slavic tongue. However, I did notice something particularly singular about the taller, towheaded, fellow. His eyes appeared to be of two different colors. After my glass was replenished, I slid back to where Holmes stood.

"I couldn't hear much," I confided. "They are still speaking in Russian."

Holmes nodded in reply, his eagle eyes fixated upon the two. Suddenly he gripped my forearm. "Watson, they are leaving. I am going to attempt to follow but I need you to come outside as well. If they stay together, return to Baker Street. If however, they separate, you take the bearded one," he said hurriedly and then scurried off in pursuit as the pair left the bar.

Holmes and I stepped into Aldgate High Street at the same time and a small raucous group of men pushed through us up the steps of The Black Horse. A thick fog had crept from the Thames, and like so many a London night, a vaporous shroud draped the city. A few feet away, the pair we had been observing exchanged a quick handshake and then separated, each taking off in opposite directions. I wasted no time in stepping after the goatee-bearded man, his bowler distinguishing him in profile as he was silhouetted against the grey mist.

Although the streets were not crowded, it was only with some great effort that I kept the man in sight. I hurried my step, as the murky haze necessitated that I remain much closer than is normally prudent in such an undertaking. The bearded individual strode along at a steady, if not quite hurried clip leaving Aldgate High Street for Jewry Street as he headed toward the river.

The neighborhood in which we entered was much lonelier than the busy stoop of The Black Horse and the street lamps provided little aid in my endeavor as the light from the blurry orbs seemed incapable of escaping the ravenous appetite of the fog. The clip-clop of a horse echoed behind me and it was only when the beast had come abreast that its ghostly pale coat could be made discernible from the blanketing mist. The creaky wheels of a wagon followed the animal and although the bed was piled high, I could not make out what the bulky shadow that represented the cargo might be. I was still puzzling over the freight as the wagon dissolved into the grey cloud ahead of me.

Although less than thirty feet in the foreground, the bowler silhouette was in danger of becoming indistinct, so I quickened my pace just in time to see the man make an abrupt left turn down one of the many alleyways skirting the street. I followed accordingly and no sooner had I turned the corner then I caught sight of a glint of steel slashing toward my face. I ducked defensively, crying out both in surprised alarm and due to the fact that as I dodged, my head slammed into the side of the building.

A gape opened in my coat where the blade had sliced through. The goateed attacker leapt forward, intent on making his second strike a more deadly one. Still dazed from the blow to my head, I could do little more than throw my hands up in a protective posture, awaiting the cold steel's bite upon my forearms. Suddenly through the fog of my stunned brain as well as the more literal mist that obscured the night, a shadow flew into view and after a whirl of motion I heard the metallic clatter of the weapon rattling upon the cobblestones and a simultaneous cry of pain, followed by running footsteps that quickly evaporated into the night.

"Watson! Watson, pray tell me you are alright!" the familiar voice of Sherlock Holmes cried out as the distorted image of his face appeared inches from my own.

"Holmes?" I managed, as I shook my head to clear away the cobwebs.

Holmes had already begun to probe my body for injuries as my mind regained focus with each passing second. I saw the loaded riding crop dangling from its strap around my friend's wrist as he peered through the slash in my coat.

"Thank heavens; only the slightest of scratches. It seems you have retained the reflexes of your rugby years! Can you stand?" he asked.

"I think so. I banged my head, but I'm feeling better every moment."

"You there!" Holmes called, turning to some indistinct image at the entrance of the alley. "Fetch a cab to this spot and there is a half-crown in it for you."

"Yes, sir!" a juvenile voice returned before his footfalls echoed off in the fog.

Holmes propped me against the wall and then scoured the ground. It was but a moment before he had recovered the would-be murder weapon. In the dim light he examined it as best he could.

31

"Are there any markings on it?" I asked, pulling myself to my feet.

"Ah Watson, it is good to see that you are intact. You gave me a terrible scare," he replied, betraying the fidelity few other than I had the good fortune to experience. Depositing the knife in his coat pocket he stated, "It may hold a point or two of interest, but it bears greater scrutiny back in Baker Street."

"Here you are, sir!" the young voice called, accompanied by the unmistakable sound of a carriage braking.

"Good job lad, here's your pay," said Holmes.

"I thought he was having a laugh," the cabman said. "I'm glad I took 'im seriously."

As we drove back to Baker Street I had fully recovered my senses. "Holmes, I am dreadfully glad of your arrival but what *were* you doing there? I clearly saw the tall man you were to follow head in the opposite direction."

"Indeed he did Watson, but as I started to trail him, I noticed that a man who had been across from the pub began to follow *you*."

The revelation startled me. "So as I was following the bearded chap, another man took up after me?" I repeated in some disbelief.

"I suspected that he was protection for the fellow you were following-- I suppose we should simply refer to him as Stephan since the other fellow in the pub, the one with the mismatched eyes, was the man I had overheard at the tearoom. Once I saw that you were being trailed I abandoned my mission, fearing the follower may intend some ill-treatment upon you."

"So, you believe they were working together," I mused.

"No longer, Watson. It was Stephan who attacked you, not this unknown man and had they been compatriots, he would have undoubtedly aided in doing you in, or at least tried to warn Stephan of my approach. However, as I sped to your aid, he melted off into the night."

As I climbed from the cab, my eye caught a glow from above. "Our sitting room is alight," I said to Holmes as he handed the driver the fare. "Someone awaits us."

"So it seems," replied Holmes as he stepped toward our doorway.

As I ascended the stair I wondered who might be in our rooms. It was obviously someone Mrs. Hudson would admit at such an hour. Could it be Gregson? Lesrade? Upon entering, it turned out that I did indeed recognize the person seated upon the sofa, but was much shocked to find the mustached man with the dark-tinted glasses from The Black Horse.

"Splendid," said Holmes, all but ignoring our visitor as he moved over to the sideboard. "Mrs. Hudson has left us some hot coffee. Care for some, Watson?"

"Y- yes," I stammered, recovering my composure. "And you?" I asked the stranger.

"Oh, no thank you, Doctor. I already have my own," he returned, pointing to a cup and saucer upon the small side-table adjacent to him.

"Here you are Watson, do take a seat," Holmes ordered, handing me the coffee.

"You were right, Mr. Holmes," the man smiled, removing his tinted glasses. "Dr. Watson does not remember me."

Holmes sighed. "Although he has come a long way, the good doctor still often sees but does not observe." Turning to me, Holmes said, "Watson, I thought those lenses might throw you, but it seems the mustache still clouds your recognition. Imagine our friend clean-shaven."

Suddenly the mystery melted away. "Mr. Ptorkin!" I all but exclaimed, recalling the young accountant we had helped clear of a knotty embezzlement frame-up about a year prior. The man's background came rushing back to me as well and I remembered that although Vladimir Ptorkin had been born and bred in London he was the child of Russian émigrés.

"So, Holmes brought you in on this to help us eavesdrop in case the pair spoke in Russian!"

34

Holmes drolly added, "Ah, Watson, it is good to see that your deductive powers have not been affected by that recent blow on the head."

"Yes," the bookkeeper grinned. "I was quite excited to participate. Mr. Holmes instructed that if those two left the pub I was to come back here and that your landlady would make me comfortable until you returned." The man's smile suddenly faded. "Doctor, are you alright?" his faced showed a degree of alarm as he pointed toward the gaping slit in the breast of my coat.

"Yes, a near miss."

"This business seems to get more sinister at every turn," Holmes interjected. "Pray tell, Mr. Ptorkin did you overhear anything that might be of interest?"

The man regained his composure and turned back to Holmes. "I don't know if it will be of use to you but I did hear something, despite their hushed tones. One phrase was repeated more than once. Several times they referred to 'the Serb's plans.'"

Vladimir Ptorkin's revelation sent Holmes into one of those pensive, reflective trances whereupon he becomes a less than hospital host. My friend lit his favorite pipe and retired to a corner chair, where he lounged, staring through the blue smoke rings at the ceiling beyond. I attempted to compensate for my incommunicative friend's apparent discourtesy, but the young accountant took no offense at Holmes's withdrawal and after he had finished his coffee, bid farewell promising further assistance if we found it necessary. I left Holmes to his contemplations and retired wondering if we had made any progress or if the knot had simply been pulled tighter.

I awoke next morning to find that Holmes had already absented himself. I hoped that his disappearance marked that he was off in pursuit of some revelation he had fallen upon during the night. Indeed, the untidy state of our sitting room suggested as much. A number of his open indexes littered the sofa and floor, and a box of newspaper clippings lay on its side spilling its contents upon the carpet.

A knock sounded upon the door. "Yes? Come in."

"Oh, Dr. Watson, I thought that I heard you milling about," Mrs. Hudson said as she entered with a breakfast tray. "Here you are," she continued, moving the coffee, toast, jam, fried eggs and rashers from the tray onto the table as I seated myself.

"Thank you, Mrs. Hudson. Would you know at what o'clock Mr. Holmes left this morning?"

"He was out about seven-thirty I should think. He took no breakfast himself, so should he return before luncheon, have him ring and I'll fix something up for him," our conscientious landlady added.

After I had polished off my meal, I crept over to the unkempt space that had passed for my friend's work area and examined the open pages of his indexes. Both the "R" and "S" volumes were present and although I scanned the pages to which they had been left open, nothing on the sheets forced a revelation. I gave a cursory sifting through the newsprint upon the floor as well, but again no headline struck me as significant. With a grunt of resignation, I left the materials as I found them and set about consulting my appointment book and stocking my medical bag with the items I would need for the morning's rounds.

As I ascended the stair that afternoon, the sonorous notes of Holmes's Stradivarius foretold that he was tapping the creative realm of his brain for inspiration towards his more scientific ends.

"My dear Holmes, on more than one occasion I have told you that you could have attained greatness as an actor, but when you put your mind to it, you are quite an extraordinary musician as well," I complimented as I hung my hat and put away my medical bag.

A smirk flitted across my friend's face. "But I am *not* putting my mind to it, Watson. I assure you that my brain is in quite another place altogether."

He began sliding his bow across the strings again in what I recognized as Mendelssohn. Upon the table sat a jack-knife, its six inch blade unfolded and locked in the open position. As I picked up the instrument I asked somewhat in jest, "Is this the knife that nearly finished me?"

Holmes quit his playing and almost carelessly propped his violin in the corner of an armchair.

"It is."

"Have you learned anything from it?" I asked, turning it over in my hands.

"It is commonplace enough, an indistinct model used by so many in daily work from the docks to the farms. Yet there are some points of interest. It has been sharpened within the last two days: was honed upon a flat stone rather than a grinder, and was whetted regularly, even if it did not need it," said Holmes relaying the unique fruits of his observational techniques.

"Why would someone sharpen a knife that does not need sharpening?"

Holmes shrugged. "Either as a habit, a ritual, or because the bearer wanted to ensure that should he need the blade to be razor sharp, he could be assured that it would be."

I depressed the lever that ran upon the back of the handle and unlocked the blade. "It seems especially loose," I commented, moving the steel back and forth.

"Yes, it has not only been oiled but worked so that a mere flick of the wrist will bring the blade to full extension. I have seen stevedores modify knives in such a fashion so that they may open it with one hand while handling freight with their other, but this one has had the hinge loosened to such an extent that it suggests that the adaptation was made more for speedy deployment then vocational convenience."

"So you believe that it is intended more as a weapon then a tool."

"I think it most likely."

"What are you doing there?" I asked, noticing that a test tube had begun to boil under a burner at his chemistry bench.

"I found some curious filings between the lock and the blade. I have some little hope of identifying the substance."

"Did you learn anything in your researches last night?" I motioned toward the indexes that still lay about.

"I had hoped to identify a reference to anyone known by the appellation *The Serb*," said he.

"Did you find any?"

He shook his head. "There is a Russian-born thief called Antonin Bulshoff who has gone by *The Serf*. It was not a bull's eye, but it was at least upon the paper."

"Perhaps Mr. Ptorkin misheard Stephan and his cohort. Perhaps *The Serf* is what was actually said."

"It is unlikely. The two words do not sound similar in Russian. Although Watson your suggestion struck me as well since they might have intertwined some English into their dialogue. To be safe I followed up the lead nonetheless. However, Bulshoff is currently incarcerated in Newgate, so I doubt those two are privy to any of his plans."

He began sliding his bow across the strings again in what I recognized as Mendelssohn.

Chapter 4

Sherlock Holmes was agitated. It is commonly known by those who have read my chronicles that my friend's energy is at its apex when given a deductive problem to solve but at the moment Holmes was like a fully coaled ship with a fouled compass. The great detective was eager for action but was having difficulty re-acquiring the scent. We of course had been afforded some direction by Holmes's determination that the dead man was a Russian and that he had been murdered. However, the only tangible thread we had obtained slipped through our fingers when my would-be assassin escaped into the night. Holmes had met with no success tracing "The Serb" and was at present in and out of our rooms at all hours, in all manner of disguise, haunting those East End establishments that might draw Russians into their orbit. Unfortunately, not only had he been unable to spot any of the familiar figures from the case, he had likewise acquired no new information from his interactions with the Russian community.

"Is Mr. Holmes in?" a lad asked when I opened our door.

"He has just returned," said I, admitting the dirty-faced urchin.

A moment later my associate emerged from his bedchamber having transformed himself from a dockworker back into the Victorian gentleman of Baker Street.

"Ah, Calhoun," Holmes greeted with some anticipation. "Any success?" he asked as he fastened his cuff.

"Not a bit Mr. Holmes," he shook his head sadly. "We'll keep at it if you want though, sir."

"Yes, pray do so," he replied, pressing a few coins into the boy's palm.

"Thank you, sir," the boy returned. "I'll tell the others to get back to work," could be heard from the stair as he was already moving to continue his mission.

"So you have deployed the irregulars, eh?"

"Yes, Watson. Those two dozen or so eyeballs have been scouring the East End for anyone meeting the description of our three known players. I am almost glad that he had nothing to report this time. Yesterday he had me waste the better part of the night chasing down a false lead. Although I have given very specific descriptions I am afraid that a mere verbal sketch of those men presents a difficulty for the lads."

"There can be few Russian-speaking men with mismatched eyes roving London."

"True, but a tinted pair of glasses and a buttoned lip are all that would be required to mask those features."

The words were barely out of Holmes's mouth when another knock sounded upon the door. "It is Gregson," I called back over my shoulder as I opened the portal.

The tall, pale, tow-headed officer removed his hat as he entered.

"Mr. Holmes, I'm glad that you're in."

"Do sit down, Inspector. A single malt? An Irish fellow for whom I did a service forwarded us a bottle out of gratitude."

"Yes, Mr. Holmes I could do with a drink, thank you."

"So what brings you around?" Holmes asked as he handed the officer the glass he had just filled at our sideboard.

"I was checking in to compare notes with you on that fellow we found by the railway platform."

"I had hoped as much," said Holmes as he seated himself upon the sofa and I took the place next to him.

"I have been all over the East End, but have not turned up a single thing," Gregson said after a sip of whiskey.

"Ha!" Holmes laughed. "It does not look as if you have much to compare."

Gregson flushed. "I suppose you are right. I was hoping that you have had some success to make up for my own deficiencies."

"Well Inspector, our ship has sailed farther than your own but it appears that we have run upon a sand-bar. I have deployed my force of irregulars in an attempt to get us re-floated."

Although Holmes often preferred to keep his own counsel when investigating a case, he was overly open with Gregson. He related how he had overheard the Russians discussing the dead man and thus had learned that his name was Boris and that he had planned to meet with a man named Stephan. Holmes further explained how one of the men he eavesdropped upon was meeting this same

Stephan and told of our efforts to learn more at that meeting as well as the attack made upon me and what we had gained from Holmes's spy, Mr. Ptorkin.

Gregson became animated, pulled his notepad from his breast pocket and began to race his pencil-point across the pages. "The Serb's plans…" he muttered. "I will run this alias, if alias it be, through our files. With all respect to your own indexes Mr. Holmes, it is possible that we have some information you do not."

Holmes nodded his acceptance.

"And what of the filings you found in the knife?" the inspector asked. I leaned forward expectantly as I had yet to hear the results of my friend's analysis.

"They were metal shavings, I suspect from a machine shop."

"Ah," said Gregson. "So our man may be a machinist. I'll look into the works, starting in the East End."

Holmes sighed. "I have already drawn a blank upon that score."

"It will do no harm to double check," said Gregson, pointing a finger into the air in a momentary break from his scribbling. "So Mr. Holmes, do you suspect these Russians from the pub are the ones who murdered this Boris fellow?" he asked, looking up from his pad.

"That remains to be determined," said Holmes, refilling the inspector's glass. There are at least two sets of players in this game as the man who followed Watson was not in league with this Stephan who attacked our good doctor."

Gregson grunted assent as he sat meditative for a moment, as if digesting all Holmes had told him. Abruptly he stood saying, "Well, thank you for your hospitality. I will see if I can make any headway in identifying *the Serb*, locating this Stephan, or finding a clue to either of them at any of the metal works in the city."

"You were very forthcoming with Gregson," I said after the inspector had departed.

Holmes shrugged. "I saw no harm in bringing him up to date. Who knows, Watson? The CID's resources are more vast than my own. They may be able to at least roust our prey by beating the bushes."

It was one of those dreary, drizzly London days and my professional business had taken me to Pall Mall near Charles II Street. I had met Mr. Sabastian Trosley during one of our previous adventures. My readers will not recognize the name as his case, though involving a valuable family artifact, possessed none of the unique and singular characteristics that denote the exploits I select to present for public consumption. Nonetheless, in helping Holmes solve his dilemma I gained the man's trust and respect in sufficient quantity that he asked my frequent consultations concerning his diabetic condition.

I had just finished with the patient and opened my umbrella as I stepped from the residence. As I moved toward the curb in an effort to hail a cab, I was shocked to see the tall, fair-haired

Russian with the mismatched eyes approaching from down the street. His head was angled downward against the rain but still I tilted my umbrella slightly forward to hide my face. I was not sure if he would recognize me or not, but thought it prudent to hide my features as a precaution. The man had no umbrella himself, but wore a waterproof brown mackinaw and a dusky wide-brimmed slouch hat. My pulse rose in excitement at the lucky prospect of chancing upon one of our apparent adversaries. With an eager anticipation, I ignored the cab that had pulled up and made off after my quarry.

It was afternoon before I made it back to Baker Street. I raced up our steps to find Holmes upon the floor sifting through a pile of papers. I consigned my umbrella to the bin and hung my slicker and bowler upon the rack.

"What have you there?" I asked with a mischievous smirk as I stowed my medical bag.

"Nothing of import I'm afraid," he replied morosely. "I vaguely remembered a reference in a *Times* article from a month or so past, but as it turns out, it has no bearing on our situation."

"That is unfortunate," I said, sitting upon the sofa, the smile still upon my face. "It is propitious then that I have had some success. I ran across that tall light-haired fellow you had endeavored to trail from The Black Horse."

For the first time, Holmes looked up from his papers and I shall forever cherish the expression upon his face.

"My dear Holmes," I chuckled. "Take a seat and I shall tell you all about it."

Holmes recovered, laughing, "Watson, you are indeed a treasure. I am eager to hear tell of your adventure," he said, pulling himself into the opposite seat and assuming a cross-legged disposition like an attentive Budda.

"I was attending to Mr. Trosely in Pall Mall when I happened upon the fellow upon the street. He did not place me and I fell in behind him."

Holmes closed his eyes and leaned back in the chair, resting his elbows upon the arms and pressing his fingertips together. "Pray continue, Watson."

"I was not certain that the man had any idea who I am. The attack by his friend may have just been upon the shadow who was trailing him that night, but I thought it best to take no chances and remain as incognito as possible. The rain was not heavy, but sufficient enough that I was not out of place with my open umbrella, which provided an excellent blind, hiding my features from view."

Holmes nodded his approval.

I continued, "He headed up Charles II Street to St. James Square where he proceeded across the square diagonally in the direction of Duke Street. Upon exiting St. James, he crossed to the Library."

"He entered the building?" Holmes asked, opening one eye.

I nodded and Holmes waved his hand, indicating that I carry on with my story.

"I followed him inside and watched from a distance as he disappeared into the stacks. I hastily placed my umbrella in the bin and hung my coat. I had no place to leave my medical bag, and entrusted it to a young clerk behind the counter. Stealthily I circumnavigated the row into which he had vanished and approached from the far side. I was able to screen myself behind a corner and peek around to view our man."

"How far apart were you and he?" Holmes interjected.

"About fifty feet."

"Continue," Holmes grunted.

"I watched as he pulled a volume from the shelf and leafed through it. He paused at a particular page and then abruptly replaced the book and left the stacks. I was startled at the haste with which he moved and hurried after him.

"Hold, Watson. Did he remove anything from the book? A note perhaps?"

"No Holmes. I am sure that he only looked inside."

"Pray continue."

I grabbed my umbrella as he made straight for the exit and although it was still raining, merely threw my coat over my arm and scurried after him. As I stepped through the doorway, I looked around anxiously to ascertain in which direction the man was moving. As I marked him, over my shoulder I heard the frantic calls of the library clerk. The young fellow ran after me with my medical case, thinking he was doing me a service as I was forgetting the bag. Of course my plan had been to retrieve it later. I tried to continue after the Russian but the eager librarian grabbed my arm in his misconception that he was acting in my benefit. I saw a look of alarm upon the Russian's face before I turned to ward off the clerk however by the time I was rid of him, the man had vanished."

Holmes gritted his teeth, and exhaled in disgust. "What did you find in the book he had been examining?"

"Sadly, I am not sure which book it was."

Holmes abruptly stood and began to pace. "Watson, I cannot understand you. You return here with news that you thought I would find welcome but what have we gained? Absolutely nothing!" he blustered.

I reddened, realizing that my friend was absolutely correct. My desire to jibe Holmes with my "progress" had clouded the reality that my efforts had produced nothing tangible.

He thrust his hands into his pockets and continued walking back and forth in silence for a full minute. Suddenly he stopped. "Can you identify the area from the shelf?"

"Yes, I am sure that I can."

"The color and size of the text?"

"All of the volumes in that area were of the same hue and many were of the same size."

Holmes tugged at the bell-pull and Billy arrived at our door almost instantly.

"Hail us a hansom if you don't mind, Billy."

"Right away Mr. Holmes," the dutiful lad returned, tipping his cap and disappearing.

"Come, Watson," he commanded, grabbing his cloak and hat. "All is not lost," he smiled, his humor brightening. "We have some work to do. We will have to peruse every book in that area. It will be tedious but it may prove productive."

Our cab left our lodgings for Oxford Street before turning onto Regent Street. The rain had picked up again and it beat a steady tattoo above our heads. A gurgle of thunder sounded somewhere to our west, but I doubt that my friend paid mind to either the peal or the downpour. He sat silent, his eyes closed. I wondered what machinations were at work in that wonderful brain. Holmes often warned against theorizing ahead of a sufficient supply of facts, but he also frequently developed a working hypothesis to guide his actions. I longed to know if Holmes had any theories as to what these Russians were up to but I knew better than to break into his contemplations.

Before long we had arrived at our destination and after paying our fair, we ascended the stone steps into that vast repository of knowledge.

"Lead the way, Watson," he stated after we had relieved ourselves of our raingear.

I snaked through the tables and across the marble floor, past a number of stacks before turning left down the artificial chasm created between a pair of towering shelves. Nearing the end of the literary tunnel I stopped to get my bearings.

"I was standing over there," I said, as much to myself as to my companion as I pointed toward the corner some distance away. I did an about face toward the shelving. "So..." I counted up three shelves from the floor and moved two shelves in from the end. "I do believe that the book came from this area." I waved my hand over a section of the cases.

Holmes examined the texts. "Fiction, authors with surnames beginning with "L," he pondered aloud.

"I would say that the volume was no smaller than this," I pointed to a book. "And no larger than this one," I said, indicating another.

"Very good, then," stated Holmes, pulling a half dozen of the thirty or so texts that fit the size parameters I had indicated. "Fill your hands, Watson. We will use that place over there," he nodded toward an empty table and without further comment lugged his burden off toward our work station.

When we were seated across from one another, Holmes opened one of the books and I followed suit. "What are we searching for, exactly?" I asked in the hushed tones required in the building.

"That, my dear Watson, I cannot say. Do you have any idea at what portion of the text he had been looking?"

I scratched my chin. "I would say the middle section of the book."

"Alright. Exclude the first and last three chapters. Starting with the fourth chapter, scan each page thoroughly. You do not have to read each page intently. I suspect there will be some markings to signify whatever it is we are after."

For an hour we drudged through this tiresome procedure but found nothing of interest in the texts. We each made another trip to the shelf and returned with more volumes of the appropriate size. Another hour had passed and my eyes were growing fatigued. I had difficulty focusing both from the blur of my vision and from the wearisome monotony of the task. Robotically I turned the sheets and I had moved from page 188 to 189 before my brain registered that something had been amiss on the previous leaf. Shaking my head to clear my thoughts, I paged back.

"Holmes!" I burst in a tone louder than appropriate for the setting. "Holmes," I repeated in a more subdued whisper, "Look at this."

My associate grabbed the corner of the book and spun it one hundred and eighty degrees so that it rested in front of him. I got up and rounded the table to look over his shoulder. Upon the page, certain letters within the text had been ticked with a small underline. Holmes withdrew the notepad from his breast pocket and quickly scratched upon it. Without a word he handed me the finished message. Anxiously I read: "Sharpoff MVD."

"MVD," Holmes repeated. "In the Cyrillic alphabet the letters MVD represent what we would translate as *Ministry for Internal Affairs.* Watson, the MVD is the home of the Okhrana--the Tsar's Secret Police."

"What does this mean?" I asked, still awed by the discovery.

"It is suggestive of one of two things. Either it is listing this Sharpoff as a contact for our mismatched eyed Russian, or if our man is no friend of the Tsar, it is a warning to him about this Sharpoff."

Suddenly, Holmes tensed. Abruptly he stood bolt upright. "Wait here," he commanded and disappeared from the table. I was both confused and mystified by my associate's bizarre behavior but equally intrigued by the message we had found. I studied the words again, speculating on whether the tall, blonde Russian and this Sharpoff were friend or foe. A few moments later, my comrade had returned and dropped a book upon the table, his finger marking a particular page. I drew a deep breath as I read the name of the author: Oliver Wendell Holmes. My friend opened the text to the page held by his forefinger: 212.

"So Boris, the dead Russian killed by the train, was *not* about to seek you out in Baker Street? The note referred to *this*?" I asked, pointing to the open volume.

Holmes however did not answer. He was busy writing down the letters underlined with the familiar ticks we had found in the previous text.

CHAPTER 5

That evening, back in Baker Street Holmes required some time to himself to consider our next move. He lay reclining in his dressing gown, drawing lazy breaths from his favorite clay pipe.

I also was in a pensive mood, reflecting on the name we had extracted from the second library text. Holmes and I both knew the name; the man was a frequent contributor to our daily supply of newspapers.

Peter Kropetsky was the son of a Russian military officer of aristocratic descent. A trained scientist, Kropetsky had published books on a wide variety of subjects from zoology to geography. His curiosity had led him astray from his patrician breeding and his open espousal of revolutionary ideals had won him two terms in the Tsar's prisons. Kropetsky found it no easier to express his views on the continent and after a stay in a French jail he crossed the channel and settled in London. The expatriate now earned a living by writing left-wing pieces for the *Times* and *Geographical Journal*. Yet, despite his alleged dedication to the lower classes, he reveled in the company of British society. Kropetsky seemed to see no hypocrisy in pontificating upon the causes of the working class as he sipped champagne amongst Britain's elite, and the Empire's nobles apparently regarded the man as less a threat than a novelty.

A good hour had passed before Holmes stirred. With his elbows he pushed himself up from his chair and placed his now spent pipe upon the mantle. Without a word, he walked over to the writing desk and dragged a sheet of foolscap from the drawer. Holmes judiciously dipped his pen and scratched out a short missive. As the ink dried he addressed an envelope and rang for our page.

"See that this is delivered, will you, Billy?" he said, handing the letter to the boy.

"Shall I post it, Mr. Holmes?"

"No, no. Deliver it personally and await a reply if the gentleman is in."

With a tip of his cap, the dutiful lad disappeared.

"You have had an idea," I stated, handing Holmes a glass of claret.

"Thank you, Watson," said he, taking the glass. "I believe that we could use a bit more information from a source whose expertise lies beyond our own. I have invited Langdale Pike for dinner at Simpsons. I would be grateful if you could attend."

"I would be glad to; if you believe he will dislodge himself from his post at the bow window of that club on St. James Street," I returned, with some sharpness in my voice.

Holmes laughed. "Your contemptuous opinion is not unfounded, Watson. Pike relishes his status as the country's chief gossip-monger but you must not think too harshly of him. His compulsive desire to learn every tidbit and rumor regarding high society has served me well before and I am hopeful that it will do so again."

That very night we shared a table at what was one of Holmes's favorite restaurants, with that strange and languid man of whom my friend had spoken. Pike treated Holmes like an old friend and Holmes in turn showed no distaste for the fellow who allegedly pulled in a four figure salary for his salacious entries into the garbage papers of London.

"I thank you for a delightful meal, gentlemen," Pike said, after he had finished his poached cod and steamed vegetables. "But I doubt you called upon me merely as a dining companion," his smirk disappeared behind the linen napkin he brought to his lip.

"Astute as ever!" Holmes returned as the waiter placed an after dinner brandy before each of us. Once the attendant had left, my friend stated the purpose for the meeting. "Mr. Pike, what can you tell us about Peter Kropetsky?"

"Hmm," the columnist pursed his lips. Langdale Pike then commenced a recitation of the man's lineage, prison terms and self-imposed exile as well as a spicy depiction of the circles of well known Britons with whom the man kept company. Sensing that Holmes and I were not satisfied with the sensational details that so drove him, he eventually broke off and asked, "Is there anything specific that you would like to know?"

"Is he sincere in his revolutionary beliefs?" Holmes inquired.

Pike chuckled. "I think intellectually he is enamored with the philosophical tenets of the far-left, especially anarchism. He was a regular at the Sunday meetings of William Morris's Hammersmith Socialist Society and you no doubt are aware of his vocal support for the striking dock workers back in '89. He despises the Tsar---that much is certain and still defiantly speaks against ourselves or even the French for that matter, allying with Tsar Nicholas. Although he is still a leading member of the Society of Friends of Russian Freedom I actually believe that now-a-days he is more charmed with his celebrity status as a radical since it gains him entrance to many of the best parties."

"You say that he is an adherent to anarchist principles," I interjected. "I assume he then advocates the violence they preach?"

"Actually Doctor, he does not, at least not publicly. He postures himself not as a true revolutionary, but as a lecturer and writer embracing certain leftist concepts. I suppose he is a bit of a contradiction in that although he champions the ends of radical thought, he claims to abhor violence as a means to achieving his vision of utopia."

"If he is being sincere," I returned.

"If he is being sincere," Pike repeated with a coy smile.

"Openly espousing violence against government would be a sure way to get deported from the British Isles, would it not?" I furthered.

"Ha!" laughed Holmes. "You may be right, Watson. This man is a known genius and it is the dimwitted firebrands who are foolish enough to let their passions spew from their lips unchecked."

Holmes and I spent another half an hour in the company of the man I still found detestable, despite my friend's admonition for tolerance.

"So Holmes," I said in the cab on the way back to Baker Street. "Was that tete-a-tete worth the effort?"

"I believe so, Watson. Although I think we shall have to dig a bit deeper into the dealings of Mr. Kropetsky."

"You are still suspicious of him then, despite Pike's reassurance that he is more talk than action?"

"Most certainly. I should be suspicious of anyone whose name appears in a secret communication; particularly when he is a proponent of revolutionary causes and we have one corpse and one near miss on our hands," he said, tapping my breast where the knife had slashed at me.

Next morning Holmes emerged from his room disheveled and in need of a shave. He wore an untidy coat with its collar turned up and a taupe cravat encircled his neck. His trousers were of the same worn fabric as the coat and the boots he had on seemed the worse for wear. As usual, my friend's efforts at masquerade were flawless as he appeared the epitome of the loafer class.

"No breakfast, Holmes?"

"Just a quick bit of respite, Watson," said he, pouring and downing a half cup of coffee before shoving a pair of scones into his pockets.

I opened my mouth to inquire about his day's mission; however the door was already closing as I uttered my first syllable.

-------§-------

"Splendid!" Holmes exclaimed, bursting into our rooms like a whirling dervish.

I had just tucked the linen napkin into my shirt and was reaching my fork to procure a slice of beef. Holmes pulled a plate and cutlery from the sideboard and stabbed a portion for himself.

"Have you not moved today, Watson? It has been nearly eight hours since I departed and here you sit in the same place as when I left!" Holmes joked. My friend's buoyant demeanor lifted my hopes that whatever his errand had been, he had met with success.

"I assure you Holmes, I earned this dinner today. My last patient was a horror. My ears are still ringing from the ill-tempered child who nearly took off my forefinger as I endeavored to examine his throat. It seems that first teeth are no less dangerous than the adult version," I replied with a smile.

"Potatoes too? Excellent!" he added, spooning a hillock onto his plate. "Thank heavens for Mrs. Hudson. I have not eaten since I saw you last."

"How you maintain your concentration under such circumstances I will never know."

"Ah Watson, the opposite is actually true. My mind is energized by fasting. Unfortunately the body eventually rebels and as it is the vehicle that carries my brain about, it must be indulged."

After he had filled his stomach a bit, Holmes asked, "Would you be averse to participating in a touch of larceny this evening?"

"What do you propose?"

"Do you recall our little criminal enterprise in the case of Milverton, the blackmailer?"

"It is to be a burglary, then?" I replied, leaning forward in intrigued anticipation.

He nodded, sipping his wine. "Today I journeyed out to Harrow, where the illustrious Mr. Kropetsky resides. After lulling about for awhile his maid came out to hang the laundry and I quickly became her confidant." He chuckled, "It is almost frightening how far a little flattery will take you with a woman of unappealing features."

"What did you learn?" I plied.

"As much as I had hoped for. There have been unfamiliar faces calling at the house, although that is not very revealing as Mr. Kropetsky enjoys holding court with whoever is interested in paying him homage. The bonanza, my dear Watson, was that she revealed that Mr. and Mrs. Kropetsky would be absent from the house tonight attending a party."

I fidgeted uneasily in my chair. "Do you think a burglary is justified?"

"We have been pointed to a character who purports a desire to dispense with our form of government. I am not sure where this case is heading Watson, but it is quite possible that our efforts would be in the national interest."

Despite a strong feeling of discomfort at the venture, I licked my lips and replied, "I have always found your judgment worthy. If you feel it necessary; then I am your servant."

"Capital!" he returned, dabbing his napkin to his mouth and refilling his glass.

Although confident of Holmes's intuition I could not shake the trepidation I felt over our illicit mission. "Will the maid not be at home? What of the other servants?"

"Remember Watson, Mr. Peter Kropetsky is an anarchist, *a man of the people*," he said in a mocking tone. "As such he cannot possibly keep minions in the household."

"How then does he employ a maid?"

Holmes laughed. "I suppose he considers it only a conditional insincerity. She lives elsewhere and is on the premises only four days out of seven."

"Perhaps Mr. Landale Pike's analysis is correct and that Mr. Kropetsky is more of a radical in theory than in practice," I smiled. "What do you hope to accomplish by breaking into his home?"

Holmes took another sip from his wineglass. "I have no clear object in mind. However I would very much like to nose around his study. I had thought of approaching him directly to question him on this business; and that may be a course of action I still take. However if this affair is as nefarious as it appears, I would prefer to see if I can gain a bit more of an upper-hand before such an interview. This man is no easy mark, Watson. By all estimations he is brilliant. Arrogant and manipulative to be sure, but these qualities make learning anything from him all the more complicated."

"Do you suspect he is at the back of all of this?"

Holmes was pensive for a moment. "If he is, I do not see the motive. He has set himself up in a nice little way here in London and despite his proclamations of being a revolutionary I find it difficult to think he would put his lifestyle in difficulty."

"Could his affection for homage and the society scene be a mere beard to advance his true radical beliefs?" I asked.

"That is an interesting thought, Watson. You do underestimate yourself at times!" he complimented. "We do not have enough data yet to make any formulations on that score. Do get together some dark apparel and those rubber-soled shoes you keep. Toss them in a sack. We will embark about nine this evening."

It was but a short rail journey to Harrow and once there we set out on foot for the Kropetsky abode. A brief carriage ride would have quickened our trek from the station however we had no interest in providing a potential witness to our caper by adding a cabman to the equation.

Twenty minutes later we were at our destination. The house was a modest brick and timber structure resting in semi-isolation atop a small, grassy knoll. Not a glimmer of light showed in the home as it sat in ghostly silence beneath a moonless, but star-filled sky. A small grove of beeches separated the property from its westerly neighbor and Holmes directed us into this copse.

"Alright Watson," he said above the mellow chirping of insects as he hung his coat upon a tree branch. "Let's get into the costumes you packed."

I removed the clothing from the sack, handing Holmes his share. The black outfits were no darker than the suites we currently wore, but far less constrictive as they were of woven cotton fiber. After slipping on our rubber soled shoes, I handed Holmes a black silk hood into which I had cut two round eye-holes. My partner pulled the article atop his head like a hat.

"Aren't you going to mask your face?" I asked.

"Oh, we can pull them down hastily enough should the need arise, but it appears that we are quite safe."

I aligned the eye-holes forward and then placed the item upon my head in the same fashion as my colleague.

Holmes reached into the bag and removed a dark lantern. "Follow me, Watson," he hissed with an exuberance that betrayed either his love of adventure or secret regret that he had not chosen to employ his talents in a criminal career.

We skirted the wooded area and then scurried to the side of the house. I mimicked Holmes as he edged his way along the siding and around the corner. When he reached the back door, from his waistband he pulled the small leather case that contained his burgling kit. I know not which of the implements he removed but a second later he was huddled over the lock and a quarter-minute beyond that, the door creaked open.

We crept into the darkened kitchen where Holmes struck a match and slid it under the shade of the lantern before pushing the extinguished Lucifer-stick into his pocket. Lifting the cover for the briefest of intervals was all that Holmes needed to ascertain the way through the room. He gently tapped my arm and then tugged at my sleeve, indicating that I should follow him. Despite the house being abandoned, we moved as noiselessly as possible and Holmes let escape the lantern-light in a most miserly fashion as he led the way down the hallway. Our progress was slow and measured as my partner gave a quick examination into each room from the hallway. It was not until we were near the front of the house that he located the study.

We slipped into the room, maintaining our silence. Holmes quickly glided over to a sturdy oak desk that sat in front of an impressive wall of books. My friend rested the lantern on the desk and lifted the shade enough to emit a thin sliver onto the desktop. He moved around the work station and pulled the leather chair forward to take a seat. Unexpectedly we both froze in horror. From the corner of the room came the unmistakable hiss of a match being struck and suddenly the glare of a lamp illuminated the room.

"Mr. Holmes," the Russian-accented voice said in a calm, suave, manner. "And I presume this to be Dr. Watson."

CHAPTER 6

Seated in a corner chair rested a man closer in age to sixty than fifty. The top of his head was devoid of hair but the long strands of grey and white that ringed his crown reached down to his shoulders and a beard of smoky hues stretched to his breast. The lenses of the small round spectacles he wore shone like two glowing moons from the reflected light of his lantern.

"If you don't mind," he said in a composed, even tone, "come and sit closer. Neither my eyes nor my ears are what they once were." He gestured toward two chairs that were near the one he occupied.

The icy tremor that had run up my spine when the match was struck had not subsided and I stood mouth agape. When I recovered, I gave Holmes a sideways glance, wondering if we should bolt. My friend employed his unique powers of mind-reading and replied to my thoughts with a slight shake of his head. Instead, he stood and approached the chairs offered by the master of the house, pulling the stocking cap from his head as he went.

"Do be so kind as to light the gas on your way over, will you Doctor?" said Mr. Kropetsky.

I did so and joined Holmes in the seats opposite the Russian exile. I sat in surly, embarrassed silence and although I could not decipher my friend's thoughts, the expression on his face and the uncharacteristic stillness of his lips betrayed that if he were not as mortified as I, he was at the least extremely displeased.

"Mr. Holmes, I have always heard that you were on the side of the law. Have you forsaken those principles and become a member of the criminal class?" he questioned, extinguishing the lantern.

"One might ask you a similar question, sir. You are said to be a revolutionary, yet you dine far more frequently with Britain's elite than with its proletariat."

The man chuckled quietly. "You know, gentlemen. I have spent time in prison. It is not pleasant in the least. Should I raise the alarm, it would not be long before you too would add the title of convict to your resume."

I sat fearfully silent but I could see that Holmes's posture had relaxed and he had regained his wits completely.

My friend smiled, replying, "Oh I doubt that, Mr. Kropetsky. I have done some little bits of service for this country in the past and I find it likely the echelons of power would intercede on our behalf; particularly when I explained the reason for my actions."

"And that would be?" asked Kropetsky as he opened a mahogany case that sat on the side-table next to him and offered us each a cigar. Following Holmes's example, I accepted and the three of us lit the expensive brand.

"Why, trying to thwart an anarchist plot of course," replied Holmes with his usual cavalier demeanor.

The Russian smiled coyly and his eyes twinkled. "Mr. Holmes, I am a scientist and a journalist. No, I believe that the constabulary would side with me, should I summon them."

Holmes shrugged his shoulders. "Shall we find out?"

Kropetsky began to rise from his chair and then fell back into it. He pursed his lips. "I have an idea. Perhaps I could ignore the flagrant felony you've committed if you credit me this favor I am doing you."

"How do you mean?" I interjected, desirous that the police not be called.

"Well, I do like it in this country and if my name were to come up in any wicked connotations you might return my generosity by speaking up on my behalf."

Holmes drew deeply on the cigar, and then looked at it in admiration before replying to the request. "Well Mr. Kropetsky, I could and would do so if I believed that you were not a party to any insidious actions. However I will not be blackmailed, nor could I possibly give a blanket assurance. Your conduct will always determine my opinion of you. If that is your condition for not raising the alarm, I only hope that the officers do not arrive before I have had the opportunity to finish this most excellent cigar."

Holmes had been right when he advised that this man's brilliance would make him formidable and I was held in near awe as these two intellectual tacticians maneuvered like a pair of chess grandmasters.

The Russian smiled. "Perhaps I can convince you that I am no threat to the English."

"Perhaps," Holmes returned. "How did you know that we were going to pay you this visit?"

"Ah Mr. Holmes," he chuckled quietly. "When I noticed a man paying so much attention to our maid out there on the back lawn, I knew that some skullduggery was afoot. She may be the ugliest woman in the county. It was easy enough to determine from her what information she had let slip. I did not know it was you of course until I threw the lantern-light upon you. I have seen your photograph more than once during my time on your island."

"Now it is my turn, Mr. Holmes," he continued. "What would bring you to my home? Why would you suspect that I was part of some--*plot*?"

"Your name appeared in a coded message associated with those we have been tracking," said Holmes bluntly. "Have you not met Stephan, here in this very room?"

"My dear Mr. Holmes, just because someone mentioned me in some correspondence you believe that I had an audience with this... what is his name again? Stephan? What would make you think so?"

"Your tea service," Holmes waved his hand toward the tray on a side table. "The cups have been used recently and not yet been cleaned. The slices of lemon upon the saucers denote that the drinkers were Russian. We Britons do not add lemon; that is a Russian custom."

The devilish smile returned to Mr. Kropetsky's lips. "I meet with a great many people Mr. Holmes, some of whom are natives of my homeland. Is this Stephan a party to this anarchist plot of which you speak?

"Not only that, my dear sir," Holmes returned, "He nearly murdered my friend and colleague here," he motioned toward me with his cigar. "Do you deny meeting with him?"

The Russian scratched the top of his bald head. "No, I do not deny it, Mr. Holmes. I do not know if Stephan is his actual name but he did indeed seek an interview with me."

"What is it he wanted?"

Kroetsky placed his cigar in the ash tray and removed his glasses. He pulled a handkerchief from his breast pocket and began to clean the lenses. "I suspect he wanted much the same thing as you do-- to determine the depth of my commitment to anarchism. Oh, he professed to merely be an admirer--and in a manner much less skillful than your own--attempted to probe me on my dedication to the principles I have espoused. You know gentlemen; your government was on the right track back in the Crimean days. Where has that animus toward the Tsarist regime gone? Now your army is in collaboration with Nicholas's against those Boxers in China and is even speaking of a new economic agreement with his government." He shook his head in disgust.

It seemed that the man could not completely check his hatred for the Romanov dynasty despite his attempts to assuage Holmes's suspicions.

"Did he attempt to bring you into his circle?" asked Holmes.

Replacing his eyeglasses, he replied, "Oh no, nothing so blatant as that. In fact, I suspect that I rather put him off when I held that the best method for exacting change was through conversion of public opinion, which in turn would determine elections, and result in the transformation of government. He, like so many on the far left, naively believes that violence is the only means to alter a political system."

"I should like to speak with this Stephan myself. Where might I find him?" my friend asked.

"I assure you that I would not know, Mr. Holmes. He sought me out, not the other way around."

"Did you know Boris?" Holmes queried.

"Boris?" his eyebrows went up. "I have known a good many in my time. To which are you referring?"

Holmes must have gauged from Kropetsky's reaction that he did not know the man killed at the railway station as he let the matter drop. Rather, he asked, "We are also interested in someone known as *The Serb*. Do you know anyone who uses that appellation?"

"Personally, no. But I do recall hearing some mention of the term at one of the parties I recently attended..." He pursed his lips in thought and sat silent for a moment. "I am sorry, Mr. Holmes, I cannot recall from whom I heard the name, nor even at which party. However, at the next one I attend, I will pose the question and see what I can learn. If I discover anything, I expect that you will tally in your score book that I have been helpful and that you might return the favor should I need a sympathetic reference."

"I would show disrespect for your intelligence if I repeated my earlier position on the subject. However be assured that any aid in helping the British government would be viewed favorably."

"Yes, of course," said Kropetsky, the sly smile returning.

"Do you know Sharpoff?" Holmes asked.

The man's brow furrowed and his smile disappeared. "The name I know, not the man. He is a member of the Okhrana and is renowned for both his fervor for the Tsar and his brutality of action. I have never seen him, and quite frankly, I hope that I never do."

After a brief stop in the grove for a wardrobe change and a brisk walk to the station, we were soon riding the train back toward the interior of London.

"I am glad that he did not call your bluff and have us arrested," said I, my voice seeped with relief.

Holmes ignored the statement and rubbed his hands together. "He has a first rate mind, Watson and is as clever as the day is long!"

"Do you think that he was truthful with us or is he really a part of this affair?"

"That is difficult to answer. He could be trying to assuage our suspicions in order to lead us down a false path. Or it is entirely possible that it is as I had originally figured; that he has set himself up nicely here with his semi-celebrity and does not wish to upset that."

"You seemed to be overly open with him."

Holmes waved his hand. "I revealed nothing that he would not have already known if he is indeed involved, and they won't be using the coded library books any longer after you were marked." He rubbed his hands together again and smiled as a famished man might look at a roast goose and said, "Watson if he is not in this, I almost hope he is taken up in another crime. I would very much like to cross swords with that man."

-------§-------

"Thank you, Doctor," Gregson said, accepting the tumbler of brandy.

"And you, Holmes?"

"Yes, Watson. Thank you."

"So, Gregson," Holmes turned to the inspector, "Lestrade does not believe that the man was murdered?"

"No Mr. Holmes. He feels that the case is a clear example of death by misadventure."

Holmes smiled. "I therefore take it that you have not shared the information I conveyed at our last meeting."

The CID man chuckled. "You know Mr. Holmes, he was so haughty about it, I decided not to enlighten him."

I joined in the amusement over allowing the stiff Lestrade to believe he had solved the fatality. "If he contends it was an accident, how does he account for the man's missing billfold?"

"Oh, he believes that the chap's near empty flask is a clear indication of his inebriation and that a man drunk enough to fall in front of a speeding train, is intoxicated enough to forget his wallet as well."

"And I suppose he likewise blames vodka for his ascending a platform where no train would be stopping at that hour," I grinned.

"Precisely," Gregson returned, before sipping at his brandy.

"What is his explanation about the message concealed in the man's shoe?" I queried.

"After I told him that you did not know the man, he was satisfied that he may have desired to seek you out over some unrelated matter and not having a billfold, placed the note in his shoe for safekeeping."

"Any success in your machine shop search?" Holmes asked Gregson.

The inspector shook his head. "Not yet Mr. Holmes. Although I am not through. And you? Have there been any other developments on your end?"

Whether Holmes would have related our illicit entry into Mr. Kropetsky's house or the interview that followed, I will never know as a sudden rap on the door interrupted the conversation.

"Mr. Holmes!" the breathless street urchin belched, entering without invitation. "We've found 'im!"

Holmes raised an eyebrow but maintained his composure asking, "To whom are you referring, Calhoun?"

"Why the Russian bloke! The tall one, blonde, thinning hair on top..."

Holmes deposited his glass upon the side table and leaned forward. His mouth opened but the youth cut him off by continuing.

"... the one with the left eye blue and the right one green!"

"Where?" Holmes asked, jumping to his feet and dashing over to grab his coat and hat.

"Well, Brooks and me saw him in Whitechapel Road. He was buying an apple at the green grocer."

"Take us there," Holmes commanded, handing me my own hat and coat.

"He's not there now, sir."

We froze in place as a dejected feeling settled in my chest.

"But we trailed him sir, and Brooks is outside his door now. If he leaves, Brooks will be after him."

"Splendid work, lad!" Holmes clapped a hand upon his back. "Care to join us, Inspector?"

"I wouldn't miss it for the world!" Gregson boomed, placing his bowler upon his head. "Lead the way!"

In a matter of moments the four of us were inside a carriage en route to Whitechapel. As we raced toward the East End, Gregson and I spoke excitedly about the prospect of confronting the elusive Russian but Holmes sat peering out of the window, merrily humming Tchaikovsky's *Waltz of the Flowers*.

The boy directed the driver to turn off of Whitechapel Road at Adler Street and then left on Commercial Road. Here he had us snake through a number of small lanes whose names escaped me although it was evident that we were working our way closer to the river.

"Calhoun," Holmes said, interrupting his humming. "Have the driver let us off a few blocks away from our destination. I do not want to alert the man by pulling right up to his door."

"Here. Stop here!" the mop-headed youth yelled to the driver.

As the coach braked to a halt my companion discontinued his self-serenade and he fairly leapt through the door, all energy and motion. He had thrust the fare into the driver's hand before Gregson and I had even alighted.

"Which way?" Holmes nearly barked at the boy as the fire of stimulation danced in his grey eyes.

"This way, sir! Follow me!"

The walk was a brisk one that took us through some of the most unsavory blocks the city had to offer. The great metropolis of London was by nature mottled with the heavy, choked atmosphere produced by so many millions living in such proximity. However in these cramped, poverty-stricken neighborhoods the dirty, oppressive labyrinth gave the impression that we had been swallowed whole by the city itself and were now passing through its entrails.

"In here gentlemen," Calhoun said, ducking through the doorway of a dilapidated brown brick tenement building. The boy led us up four flights of stairs and down a dark, squalid hallway that faced the rear of the building. "There's Brooks," he stated, pointing toward a small head that had peaked from a recessed alcove.

"I take it he's still in there?" Holmes quietly asked, rubbing his hands together as the boy stepped from his hiding place.

"Yes sir, Mr. Holmes."

"Anyone else?"

"Not unless they were already in there, sir. No one has come since I've been on guard."

My companion handed each lad payment and whispered. "Well done men. Be off with you, then. Quietly, though." He gave them a salute, which they returned before gently scampering back down the hallway.

Holmes put his ear to the grimy door. He nodded and waved Gregson and I forward. We could hear some traces of movement inside. My friend raised his hand and knocked. Silence suddenly reigned behind the door but just as abruptly we heard a hurried commotion beyond and Holmes motioned to Gregson.

"Scotland Yard! Open this door at once!" the inspector bellowed.

The noise within continued for another ten seconds and then all was silent. Gregson tried the knob, and finding it locked, banged heavily upon the wood.

"We must break it down," Holmes stated with grave eagerness. "But be careful, we do not know what waits within."

Gregson and I threw ourselves against the barrier. On the third attempt, the frame of the jam nearest the knob splintered and the door caved inward, separating from its top hinge as the inspector and I tumbled into the room. Holmes leaped over and past us. As Gregson and I clamored to our feet we saw that the chamber was empty. Holmes was at the grate, stamping on a litter of papers that had been set afire.

"The window!" I yelled and the inspector and I scurried across the room. Holmes was right behind us as we peered through the open aperture.

"There!" said I, pointing. Ten feet to the right, the Russian stood on the ledge, a frantic look in his mismatched eyes.

"Come back here, now!" commanded Gregson, "By order of Scotland Yard!"

The ledge ended not five feet beyond where the man stood, so I saw no alternative to Gregson's decree. The wily Russian looked about anxiously. The inspector began to repeat his command but mid sentence the desperate fugitive jumped out into space.

CHAPTER 7

Horrified, I instinctively stretched my hand out to grab the man even though he was far beyond my reach. I next expected to see our quarry as a broken, bloodied mass on the pavement below. However he had leapt across the alleyway toward the adjacent building and in a tremendous stroke of luck, met his objective of grasping the drainpipe that ran vertically down the corner of the brickwork. The man was hardly out of danger though. Not only was he four stories above the pavement, but his impact had dislodged the rainspout from its moorings and the metal conduit groaned loudly as it began to sway.

I stood staring, dumbstruck as the man hung between life and death. His legs kicked violently as he urgently sought some foothold upon the pipe or the brick wall to which it had been affixed mere moments before. Just as I expected the Russian to plummet to his doom, the pipe fortuitously bent cleanly in half, softly lowering him not five feet from the ground. With some exclamation in his native tongue, he let go and dropped to earth.

Before I could utter a sound, I heard Holmes's footfalls pounding down the hallway. Gregson and I looked at one another and shook off our awe. Without a word we sprinted off after Holmes.

By the time Gregson and I reached the bottom of the stairs, we were both winded. Still we darted through the building's door and ran around through the alleyway in time to catch a glimpse of Holmes disappearing behind the far corner. I slapped Gregson's arm with the back of my hand and pointed toward the vanishing detective and we were off again. The chase took us through a maze of alleys. At times we caught fleeting glimpses of Holmes while at other moments we were forced to halt and listen for the pounding footsteps that set us off again in the proper direction.

I was nearly spent when we emerged from a narrow passageway to find ourselves not far from a small, dilapidated wharf that protruded precariously out into the Thames.

"There!" said I, pointing toward the figure of my friend bent over an old and wholly unfit rowboat.

"Holmes!" Gregson panted as we rushed up. "Have you lost him?"

"Only for the moment," my friend replied over his shoulder, pointing out into the river. There, downstream lay the fugitive, pulling hard upon the oars of a stolen skiff.

Holmes had extracted his multiplex knife and had just sawed through the rigid, ancient tar-covered rope that had lashed the craft to a piling for what had probably been no less than a decade.

"Get in, gentlemen," Holmes ordered.

"In that?" I asked, exasperated at the prospect of heading out in the leaky, worm-eaten craft.

"Make haste, man! He is with the tide and gains every moment!" my friend retorted in agitation.

Holmes was already in the prow and Gregson as I clamored into the sorry vessel. Much to my surprise the boat did not sink under our weight.

"Take an oar and pull!" Holmes instructed.

Side by side, the inspector and I each got behind a handle. Out we went into the swift current, a whirling eddy spinning us in the proper direction as we cleared the ramshackle pier. Despite the exhaustion that still plagued me from the long and winding chase to the riverside, my adrenal glands pumped furiously at the thrill of seeing our prey a mere hundred yards ahead. Gregson and I rowed like a pair of demon oarsman traversing the river Styx.

"Good work, men!" Holmes called. "We're gaining!"

The inspector and I had our backs to the Russian as we pulled feverishly at the oars but I sneaked a glance over my shoulder to see that the distance between us had been cut in half. Five minutes more and we were even closer.

"Ah, he's stopped rowing. It seems as if he is resigned to give in," Gregson said after turning for a peek ahead.

Holmes was strangely quiet, leaning forward in the bow, his hands holding each side of the gunwales. We were within twenty feet of our quarry when my companion spoke.

"He's fiddling with something..." said Holmes in a tone that betrayed curious concern. Suddenly a thud sounded from within our own craft.

"Jump! Jump out, now!" the horror in Holmes's voice commanded that we act immediately but I needn't have ejected myself since as my companion sprang from the boat, he dragged me along with him. Seconds later the cool murk of the river enveloped me. I clawed at the water, abruptly bobbing to the surface, coughing and sputtering. A moment later Holmes and Gregson broke water next to me. Our leaky little craft drifted speedily away, a thin wisp of black smoke rising from within. Suddenly a spectacular explosion reduced the wooden boat to splinters. Beyond, the Russian paddled onward farther and farther from our grasp.

As I dragged myself ashore, Holmes emerged. Sopping wet, he trod over to a large, petrified piling that sat lengthwise in the mud, exposed by the retreating tide. He took a seat upon the ancient timber and leaned forward, elbows upon his knees. Gregson followed and after I caught my breath, I joined them.

"A grenade?" Gregson asked, removing his coat and wringing it out.

"More of a small pipe-bomb," Holmes replied. The fuse was short and it rolled under the seat or I would have attempted to throw it back out."

"Well Holmes," I stated, "You were correct in declaring this business 'sinister.' I have now twice been nearly killed during this case."

Holmes grunted in reply. "Inspector, I suggest that you find a callbox and although I think it probably futile, try to put out an alert along the docks downriver. "Watson," said he, turning in my direction "I will meet you back in Baker Street as soon as I can."

"But where are you going?" asked I. However as Holmes walked off, a dripping, soaked mess he was already so absorbed in thought that he did not answer. He disappeared over a bulkhead as Gregson and I labored to our feet to head to our respective destinations.

It took me three tries and the promise of an extra crown before I could find a cabman willing to have me as a fare. It was a warm day, but a humid one as well so by the time I was back in Baker Street, I was nearly as damp as I had been when I crawled from the Thames. As I emerged from my bedroom cleaned and clothed in a fresh suit, I felt much improved, but the adventure had left me rather fatigued and as I reclined upon the sofa waiting for Holmes to return, gravity began tugging at my lids and I drifted off into the realm of slumber.

I awoke with a start. Whatever dream I had been having fled my memory as I regained consciousness. Although I could not remember the content, it had been an emotive one as a sense of angst still weighed upon my chest and beads of sweat covered my forehead. As a sense of awareness rushed back I heard a noise and sat up to see the back of my friend, clad in fresh, dry clothes. He was seated at the table, his shoulders bent forward, engaged in some sort of an examination. Shaking my head to clear the cobwebs, I pushed myself up from the sofa.

"You've returned, Holmes? What time is it?" I asked rhetorically as I tugged my watch from my pocket to see that more than an hour had elapsed since I had lain down. "What do you have there?" I furthered, coming closer to my friend.

"These are the remnants of what the Russian tried to destroy before we burst in," said Holmes, sifting through a pile of charred paper fragments.

"Ah. Anything of value?" my curiosity piqued, I took the seat next to my companion.

"He did a rather thorough job, I'm afraid," replied Holmes. "He spilled some lamp oil on the documents before applying the match."

"Did the room hold no other clues?" I asked, hoping for something further than the pile of scraps.

"Nothing of note. Some discarded tin cans and empty bottles. It appears that it was used only as a meeting place. The landlord said that the room was unrented, so there is no chance of tracing them in that direction."

Holmes peered through his magnifying lens at each blackened scrap as he delicately maneuvered the fragments with a small pair of tweezers. Sadly, each one he examined showed nothing more than ebony ash. I pulled my handkerchief and was about to remove the perspiration from my brow when Holmes erupted.

"Halloa! Halloa!" he exclaimed.

"What? What is it?"

"Watson, I do believe we have something here," he said, darting over to his chemical bench. I followed and peered over his shoulder as he dipped an artist's paint brush in a bottle of solution and subtly dabbed at the one inch fragment he held in the tweezers.

At first the scrap appeared no different than the others but upon closer examination I noticed that it had escaped total emersion in the fire and had a curious bluish tint to it. Holmes retrieved another brush and plunged it into a second vial of chemical liquid. Again he painted the piece of paper.

"Look here, Watson!"

"But... what is it?" asked I.

"Exactly what it represents I cannot say but this is definitely a part of a blueprint or schematic. Although there isn't much here," he said gazing through his magnifying lens, "this was definitely a diagram for some type of machine."

Next morning Holmes disappeared, confiding that he was taking the scrap to Hatherley, Finch, and Marker; an engineering firm in which one of the partners had enlisted Holmes's aid in the past. I sat enjoying a pipe of a fine blend of Dutch tobacco considering the link between the metal filings found in the knife and the recent discovery of this apparent design for some form of mechanical device. A sudden wrap upon the door roused me from my thoughts.

87

"Doctor Watson?"

"Yes, Billy?" I called as the head of our page poked into the room.

"Begging your pardon, sir but this just arrived for Mr. Holmes," he said, handing me an envelope with my friend's name neatly printed across its face.

I thanked the young man and deposited the missive upon the desk, wondering if it was one of the never ending appeals for my companion's assistance or if perchance it bore some relevance to our current problem.

-------§-------

"So they were of no aid?" I asked.

"Even though the piece was a small one, Mr. Hatherley was able to corroborate my notion that it belonged to a diagram for a machine. However neither he nor his partners could give any guidance as to what type of device it might be. In fact they were bewildered beyond reason, having seen nothing like it in all their careers."

"Oh, Holmes, I had almost forgotten, this message arrived while you were out," said I, retrieving the envelope from the desk.

Holmes subtly dabbed at the fragment

Holmes grabbed a knife from the cutlery set and applied it as a make-shift letter opener. Moving over to the window, he unfolded the single page document and held it to the late afternoon sunlight streaming into the room.

"Ah ha, Watson!" he exclaimed, slapping the letter with the back of his hand. "It is from Kropetsky! He has made good on his offer to keep his ears open. Perhaps he does not have crime at his heart... more's the pity," Holmes said in an aside. "He informs that he recently attended a festivity where he overheard Sir William Thompson railing about the traitorous *Serb* who recently arrived at Sebastian de Ferranti's laboratory."

"Ferranti's? The electrical engineering firm? Their laboratory is in Oldham, Manchester," said I.

Holmes consulted his pocket-watch and his mouth set in a grim line. We shall have to catch the first train tomorrow. "If you don't mind Watson, this evening clean your service revolver. Bring it to Oldham for good measure."

After a hasty breakfast we climbed into a cab and it was not long before we were walking under the Euston Arch that marked the entranceway to the rail station. The journey to Manchester ate up a good portion of the day and as we sped northward, I speculated as to whether the trip would produce the man we sought or if the effort would culminate in another dead end. I even wondered if Mr. Kropetsky might be purposely drawing us from

London for some wicked intention and if we should have telegraphed ahead for some confirmation that a Serbian had indeed recently arrived at Ferranti's. Holmes admitted that he had considered the idea but that he thought it better to make an unannounced entrance so as to catch "The Serb" unawares if indeed it was the man we were after.

Upon alighting at Manchester Piccadilly we ordered a hansom driver to take us to Ferranti's facilities in Hollinwood, Oldham. As we stepped to the curb Holmes pulled me aside.

"Watson, I will pursue this in as gentlemanly a fashion as possible. However, keep a grip on that pistol of yours. Remember that Ptorkin informed us that the conspirators repeatedly referred to *The Serb's plans*; inferring that he is behind of all of this. What his end purpose is we still do not know but his intentions are evil to be sure. If our man is inside this building, danger lies within."

Holmes presented his card and asked for Mr. de Ferranti. The clerk minding the reception desk gave a slight bow and disappeared through a wooden door, the top half of which was made of frosted glass. A moment later the clerk returned with an intelligent looking young man not yet thirty years of age. The man's sleeves were rolled up and he pulled a handkerchief from his pocket and wiped his hands before extending his right to shake our own.

"Mr. Holmes," said he "and Dr. Watson. It is indeed a pleasure. I have enjoyed reading of your adventures," he smiled in a friendly manner. I am Sebastian de Ferranti. How may I be of service?"

"Mr. de Ferranti, we are interested in speaking with a newly arrived gentleman of Serbian extract we believe to be on the premises," Holmes bluntly stated.

The electrical engineer smiled again. "I had no idea his presence in this country was common knowledge. Right this way," he said, pushing open the door with the frosted-glass window.

I was a bit perplexed by Mr. de Ferranti's reaction and was dwelling upon it as he led us down a hallway and into a room adorned with several drafting tables. The room was devoid of people save a dark-haired man with his back to us, who appeared to be scribbling away with a pencil while frequently checking and adjusting a slide-rule. Remembering Holmes's warning, I pushed my hand into my coat and wrapped it around my revolver's grip.

"Mr. Holmes, Dr. Watson," said de Ferranti when we reached the man. The Serb turned his mustached face toward us, his blue eyes fixing their gaze upon our features, "this is Nicola Tesla."

"The same Mr. Tesla who's experiments with wireless telegraphy I have read about?" Holmes asked, a bit surprised.

"The same," replied the man through a Eastern European accent.

"And who designed the power dynamos for Westinghouse?" I added.

"Again," he returned with a slight bow of his head.

"Mr. de Ferranti," said Holmes, turning toward the proprietor, "would you have an office where we could converse? This may take a time to untangle."

"But of course, this way."

As the engineering firm proprietor led the way I recalled what I knew of Mr. Tesla. Now in his mid forties, he had been born a scientific prodigy in Serbia. He studied and worked in Europe eventually migrating to America where he had been employed in the laboratory of Thomas Edison before moving on to work for Edison's rival George Westinghouse and then eventually striking out on his own. He had made significant contributions to not only all things electrical but proved to be a revolutionary inventor and physicist as well.

Mr. de Ferranti took up the seat behind his desk while Holmes, Tesla and I occupied comfortable chairs that already formed a semi-circle upon an attractive oriental carpet.

"Mr. Tesla," Holmes began, "Might I ask what you are doing here in England?"

The inventor looked at de Ferranti who smiled and nodded his acquiescence to answering the question.

"The Ferranti Corporation is contracted to build dynamos for alternating current production of electricity here in the British Isles, and I have agreed to allow some of my designs to be used. Some modifications are required and I am here making the necessary adjustments."

Holmes rested his elbows on the chair arms and began to tap his fingertips together. "Would you know why Sir William Thompson would refer to you contemptuously as *a traitor*?"

Tesla chuckled. "I assume the 'contempt' is because I am helping Mr. de Ferranti. You see, Sir William is among those who had invested heavily in Edison's direct current system and when it was proved that our system, *alternating current*, is far more efficient and useful, and we received all of the contracts he hoped for-- well you might well understand his contempt."

"And his assertion that you are a traitor?" I interjected.

Tesla shrugged. "I suppose it is because I once worked for Mr. Edison but left him and partnered with his competitor, Westinghouse in order to develop the system of alternating current."

Holmes smiled, apparently accepting the man's explanations. He dug into his pocket and stretched his hand toward the man seated next to him saying, "And Mr. Tesla, do you recognize this?"

The electrical genius took the small scrap of paper and eyed it for less than a second. "My God!" he exclaimed. "This is taken from the plans for my Electro-Mechanical Oscillator! Where did you get it?"

"What a fool I have been!" Holmes muttered, ignoring the inventor's question.

I gasped, "*The Serb's plans*! The phrase does not refer to a scheme, but to a mechanical design!" The realization had dawned on me a second after Holmes had reached the same, though unspoken, conclusion. "But..." I recovered, turning to Tesla. "What does the machine do?"

"It destroys," Tesla said quietly, as he turned the fragment over in his fingers.

CHAPTER 8

"Every material has a resonant frequency," Tesla explained. "That is to say, a reverberating frequency. If the frequency of an object can be matched and amplified, it can literally be vibrated until it breaks apart." Reading the confusion upon our faces he tried to simplify the concept. "Have you ever seen a wineglass shattered by a high-pitched tone?"

"In fact we have; Holmes do you recall we watched an opera singer perform the feat at the Exposition Universelle?"

"Indeed," Holmes replied curtly, fixing his attention upon Mr. Tesla. "Pray continue."

"The same concept may be applied to much larger items. Have you heard tell of the Angers Bridge collapse?"

"In France, mid-century?" I replied, questioning my memory.

"Yes. It was a suspension bridge over the Maine River. The marching cadence of the soldiers crossing the bridge unfortunately harmonized with the resonant frequency of the bridge itself, causing it to collapse, killing two hundred of the soldiers."

"Ah yes," I interjected, "It is the reason infantry are ordered to march out of step when crossing a bridge."

"Exactly," Tesla returned.

"And you attempted to design a device that could artificially create this effect?" Holmes interrupted.

Tesla looked at the floor. "No."   He raised his eyes to meet ours, "I actually built one."

"A functioning machine?" I asked, shocked.

The Serbian nodded. "I attached it to a girder in my laboratory, in New York. I was experimenting with it, and once I hit upon the frequency corresponding to the laboratory, the whole structure began to shake. I could not get it to shut off and had to smash it to bits with a hammer. In another few minutes the whole building would have been reduced to rubble. There was pandemonium out in the street," Telsa recalled. "Police, ambulances, fire crews... I told the police it had been an earthquake and that is all they ever knew about it."

A thoughtful stare glazed over my eyes. "It was you!" I blurted, turning to Tesla. "I read about a freak earthquake in New York City in the newspaper. But it had not been an earthquake at all... it was your machine!"

Tesla smiled grimly and shrugged his shoulders. "I destroyed the device and the plans."

"And yet those plans have obviously been reproduced," Holmes stated. "Who besides yourself might be familiar enough with the intricacies of your design to draw up a facsimile of your blueprint?"

The electrical genius pursed his lips. "That scrap undoubtedly represents a replica of my own machine. I had an assistant who was working closely with me at the time... and I have neither seen nor heard of him since. A Russian fellow named Stephan Kosovitch."

A dour expression fell upon my face but the revelation animated Holmes. He sprung from his chair and began to pace the room, hands behind his back.

"Mr. Tesla," can you please describe the man for us; physically?"

The description matched the characteristics of the one we knew as "Stephan."

"And Mr. Tesla, have you any knowledge of Stephan's (Holmes still referred to him by his Christian name as that is how we knew him) background and political opinions?"

The inventor rubbed his chin. "As I said, he is Russian; schooled in Moscow and Budapest. I am not political and insist that my men concentrate discussions on scientific pursuits while in my lab; so I do not know much about him beyond his engineering qualifications. However..." he thought for a moment. "I do believe that he mentioned that his family had endured some persecution at the hands of the Tsarist Regime and that he was resentful of the current state of affairs in his homeland."

"Mr. Holmes," interrupted Mr. de Ferranti. "If I might be so bold; what is this all about?" his voice betrayed that he had gleaned enough to know that danger lurked behind it all.

Holmes related the situation with broad strokes, stating that Russian anarchists were at large in London and that Mr. Tesla's former assistant was among them and that although we did not yet know their objective, it seemed apparent that Stephan was at work reproducing Tesla's oscillation device for some dastardly purpose.

"So this machine could conceivably bring down a building or bridge?" I asked of Tesla.

He nodded somberly.

"How long would it take?" I asked.

"Fifteen minutes perhaps," replied the inventor bleakly.

We all fell silent for a moment.

"I must ask you both to keep this information confidential," Holmes stated with authority. "Although it is unlikely the common man would believe Mr. Tesla's device to be anything but a facet of a Jules Verne story; Londoners would certainly become unsettled at the prospect of an anarchist plot in the city. We do not want a panic created. Not only would hysteria not be in the public interest, it would impede our prospects of thwarting this scheme."

Both men readily agreed.

"I gather that the machine would have to be affixed to the superstructure of the object it was meant to destroy?" asked Holmes.

"Yes," Tesla replied.

"What would be the approximate size of such a machine?" Holmes queried.

99

He spread his hands eight inches or so.

I was aghast at the possibility that such a small device could wreak that degree of havoc.

Holmes was pensive. "So if the machine were deployed it *could* be destroyed before it brought down the structure-- as you did to the one in your laboratory-- but it would have to be found quickly as you indicated that it could collapse its target in minutes. Yet given its small size, it could be nearly impossible to locate the device before it completed its task."

As Holmes was speaking, the idea of Mr. Tesla's device triggered my thoughts to drift back to my medical training. I considered the successes that had been made fighting disease through inoculation and the concept of using a virus to nullify its own potency. "Mr. Tesla," said I, "You have explained that any given object has a frequency and by attuning your invention to that frequency, the object could be virtually vibrated to pieces. Could not a countervailing device be used to cancel out the frequencies emitted from the machine being used as a weapon?" I ventured.

Tesla and de Ferranti looked at each other. "Yes, Doctor... I believe that is possible," the Serbian replied slowly, as he pondered the notion. "However it would have to be a different design; one that did not utilize the same frequencies, but rather opposing ones-- as the way letters appear backwards in a mirror. You understand?" his accented voice asked.

Before I could reply, Holmes intervened. "Watson, you are wonderful at times!" Turning toward the engineers my friend said, "Gentlemen, the good doctor has stumbled upon a solution that may save the day. Would you be willing to devise and build such a machine?"

Both men stood. "But of course!" Tesla answered for both.

"Capital!" Holmes returned. "If you succeed, the world may end up owing you a tremendous debt. Could you possibly speculate as to how long it might take?"

"Not long," Tesla answered. "I can already envision the design."

"I wonder if it might be possible for you to do your work in London," asked Holmes. "It appears whatever their target may be, it is in the metropolis and I would hate to see Tower Bridge fall into the Thames while I was on a train to Manchester to recover your invention."

"I will telegraph to London immediately; I am certain that we can use the facilities at Siemens," said de Ferranti.

"Excellent. Please do not delay an instant. Watson and I will be off immediately. Hopefully we can apprehend the fiends before they can progress any farther with their plans."

"I am surprised that you were aware of Mr. Tesla's work," I stated as our train streaked back toward London.

Holmes flashed a wry smile. "As you know Watson, I do not generally concern myself with reading that does not advance my professional pursuits. However, before you returned to reside at Baker Street I had a most singular case where electricity was used as an instrument of murder. I shall really have to give you the notes on that investigation Watson. I know how drawn you are to the grotesque cases," my friend interrupted his own thought. "In order to untangle the knot, I researched the field of electricity in some depth and Mr. Tesla's monographs were extremely helpful."

"Watson," said Holmes as the train was pulling into the station, "Could you go and see if you can find Gregson?"

"Certainly."

"If you are able to locate the inspector, kindly apprise him of the latest developments.

"Are you off somewhere else then?"

"Yes. I should be back in our rooms in an hour or two," Holmes replied without revealing his destination as he stepped onto the platform and vanished in the crowd.

"But, it's fantastic!" Gregson grunted in disbelief.

"Be that as it may, it is true. Mr. Tesla built the device and Holmes is confident that his former assistant, the Stephan we've been after, is constructing a replica."

The inspector fell into the seat behind his desk. He scratched at the hair about his temples. "So Mr. Holmes feels that these

Russians are out to knock down some edifice here in London? Why?" he asked, looking up. "How would that help them in any way against the Tsar? It makes no sense," he grumbled.

"I will admit that even Holmes is still in the dark as to their motives or their specific target. Yet he is certain that dirty dealings are afoot and he asked that I update you on our progress."

Gregson was quiet for a half minute. "Doctor, I must say that I find it hard to accept that such a machine could exist. However, my respect for Mr. Holmes forces me to suspend my disbelief. The difficulty is that if what you say is true, I must take this information to my superiors-- yet I am uncertain how I will convince them that I am not mad."

"Perhaps if they heard it from Holmes himself," I postulated.

Gregson brightened at the thought that the tale might reach his superiors' ears from someone other than himself. "Yes. Yes! Where is Mr. Holmes? Will he come in with me?"

"I do not know where he is," I replied. "He headed off on some mission of his own as soon as we got back from Manchester." Gregson deflated at the news. "If I might suggest," said I, sorry that I had given the inspector false hope, "it is your duty to lay the details before your superiors immediately. However, use the name of Mr. Holmes as you see fit and if they need further corroboration, send a message to Baker Street and I will tell Holmes to come to the Yard or if he cannot, to send a note in his own hand."

103

"And you say that Mr. Tesla is at work constructing a countermeasure to this oscillation machine?" Gregson jotted some comments on a piece of foolscap.

"Yes, he and Mr. de Ferranti are, I believe, using the facilities at the Siemens laboratory, here in London."

"I shall have to check on that," Gregson said, more to himself than to me.

"Oh, and I assume it is safe to suppose that no officer down river apprehended the fleeing Russian?" I added as I moved toward the door.

"What's that?" the inspector said. "Oh. No. We found the boat, but the devil was long gone."

"You spoke with Gregson?" Holmes asked as he burst into our rooms, tossing his hat and coat upon a chair.

"I did, although he found the idea of the oscillation device difficult to swallow and was not enthusiastic about relating our suspicions to his superiors. He hoped that you would stop around to lend your name to the story."

"There is no time," Holmes waved off the thought as he poured a glass of water from the carafe and quickly downed the contents. "I believe that a higher authority than I will serve the same purpose, however."

"How do you mean?"

"I went directly to the Diogenes Club and laid the matter before Mycroft."

Sherlock Holmes's older brother Mycroft held an unofficial position within the government and although Holmes believed that his sibling possessed even greater deductive talents than his own, the elder Holmes had not the vigor to put his gifts into the convulsive action needed as a consulting detective. However, Mycroft's aid to the government was valuable and his contacts were many.

"Did he reach the same conclusions we have reached?"

"Indeed; and thought the matter just as pressing. He even left that club of his and scurried off to Whitehall."

"That alone shows the severity of the affair," I quipped, knowing how anathema activity is to Mycroft Holmes.

"Unless I am much mistaken, we will be getting a visit from someone in the Home Office very shortly."

Within the hour a four-wheeler had braked to a stop in the street below and the quick, scampering tread of our page could be heard ascending the stairs. However, the two men who had alighted from the carriage did not wait below until Billy had presented their cards. Rather they were at the boy's heels as he knocked upon our door.

"Dr. Watson, these gentlemen want to see you. They wouldn't let me announce them," he glared over his shoulder.

"That's alright Billy. Thank you. Won't you come in gentlemen," I said to the somber looking figures.

The first man was a well-dressed chap in his mid-thirties. His hair was a chestnut brown and neatly pomaded. The tips of his mustache were waxed and he carried himself in a stately manner. His companion was tall, perhaps two inches over six feet and must have weighed fifteen stone. His chest was thick and his shoulders broad. He was bare-headed and his ginger colored hair although combed, had an unkempt feel about it. He was clean-shaven and his eyes were mere narrow slits that gave off the impression of a crafty mind.

"Good day," said the well-dressed gentleman as he removed his top hat. "I am Mr. Jeffery Downing of the Foreign Office."

I read the momentary confusion on Holmes's face as he had been expecting a representative from another cabinet post.

"And this," he said of his cohort, "is Mr. Sharpoff..."

"Of the Okhrana," Holmes interjected, pouncing upon the name we had recovered from the coded library book.

Mr. Downing gave a bit of a start. "I was going to say of The Imperial Russian Government but it seems you have information more specific than I had intended to offer."

"Gentlemen, do sit down," Holmes invited. "Mr. Downing you would do well not to attempt to hide anything from me. You are obviously here because you understand the seriousness of the

106

matter. If you are not as forthcoming as possible, any tragedy that occurs will be your responsibility."

"Of course you are right, Mr. Holmes," replied the gentlemen as he toyed with the end of his mustache. "We owe you the frankness you request. So you feel that Stephan Kosovitch is constructing a destructive machine based upon Mr. Tesla's design and that he and other Russian revolutinaries mean to inflict some mischief upon the city?"

"I had suspected as much, however your arrival, as opposed to someone from the Home Office suggests that their goal is likely not to attack a British target, unless of course it is incidental to achieving their true objective."

Mr. Downing glanced at the Russian, but the man sat in stony silence appearing to be without emotion, or possibly even interest in the conversation.

Turning back to Holmes, Downing said, "We are aware of the anarchists and we have no doubt that they are here with ill intent. However the oscillation machine was news to us. We must thank you for your diligent work in uncovering the means they are likely to employ."

Holmes leaned back in his chair. "Now gentlemen, as Dr. Watson and I have done you the service of filling in some gaps for you, pray do us the same courtesy so that we can put the entire picture into focus. What is it that has drawn both Russian anarchists and Tsarist enforcers together, here in London?"

Mr. Downing wet his lips. "What I am about to tell you must go no farther than this room." He fidgeted uncomfortably in his seat. "Three of the Tsar's representatives have arrived in London this very day. They are to negotiate a very delicate, but for the Tsar very vital, finance agreement. There is a feeling amongst economists that the western money markets are likely to contract and if Imperial Russia is not able to restructure her obligations, the country's industry will likely be plunged into a serious and prolonged crisis. So crucial are these dealings that the negotiations have been kept secret. Unfortunately a radical sect learned of the ministers' intentions, and we believe, are out to sabotage the meetings."

"And Mr. Sharpoff, here," Holmes nodded toward the stoic Russian. "He and some friends have been on the prowl trying to deal with the anarchists?"

Mr. Downing replied, "Mr. Sharpoff and another agent have been on the lookout for them, yes."

"Like the one they pitched in front of the train?" Holmes returned.

The Foreign Office man started. "One of the anarchists did fall from a train platform while being pursued by Mr. Sharpoff and his colleague…" He looked at the Okhrana agent aghast that he might have been fed a false story by the Tsar's officials.

For the first time, the Russian spoke. "Accident," he bluntly said, his lips creasing unnaturally in an attempted smile.

I recalled Mr. Kropetsky's comments about the ruthless Okhrana man and looking at his steely, narrow eyes, I concluded that the exiled scientist's assertions had not been exaggerated.

Holmes glared at Sharpoff. "Yes, and I suppose that he accidently lost his billfold and identification prior to diving in front of a speeding train. Without being able to identify the man it becomes less likely that the police could trace him and establish a motive for foul play."

The Okhrana agent shrugged.

"How many are left?" asked Holmes curtly.

"Two," the Russian blurted.

"That leaves Stephan and the blonde fellow with the mismatched eyes," I said.

"Dimitri Brusilov," said Sharpoff, naming the man.

"But," I interjected. "Why the need for Tesla's machine? Could they not just use a bomb?" I asked, knowing it had been the method employed to murder Tsar Alexander II almost two decades earlier.

Holmes answered, "Unless one could get close enough to all three ministers, it would not have the desired effect. After all, a bomb could not bring down an entire building; at least not a structure of any substantial size. With Mr. Tesla's device, one would not even need to know where in the building the targets were, and their death seems almost certain if the whole edifice fell atop them." Holmes paused. "And remember, Watson this is also

109

a terror weapon. If they can demonstrate that they can bring down a building or bridge at will, they will likely feel their demands will be given much more credence."

A grim silence fell upon us.

"Your message stated that Mr. Tesla is in the country and working on a machine that could thwart the one Stephan Kosovitch is building. Is that correct?" Downing asked.

"Yes, Mr. Tesla is pursuing that path and believes that he can construct such a device. However, there are many hazards to putting all our faith in that prospect. It would be most advantageous if we could bag our game before they are able to attempt their strike," said Holmes.

"Mr. Downing," I interjected, "We have been on this case since the anarchist we know as 'Boris' turned up dead," I narrowed my eyes toward Sharpoff, but the likely assassin sat unfazed. "We have been working with Scotland Yard, and as we speak, an inspector is briefing his superiors on as much as we knew before your arrival."

"Yes. We have dispatched a man to the Yard. I swore you to secrecy over this matter and the same oath is being extracted from the CID officers. Gentlemen, keep in mind that although we are certainly attempting to prevent a crime, there is an even larger issue of international diplomacy at stake."

Holmes closed his eyes. A few moments later his lids lifted and he asked, "I am assuming that the three Russian ministers are not only guarded, but in an undisclosed site?"

"You are correct," Downing replied. "They are being sequestered in a secret location."

"They are safe," Sharpoff stated blandly.

"Mr. Sharpoff, why did you not come to Dr. Watson's aide when Stephan launched his murderous attack?" Holmes asked in a calm voice.

The Russian did not answer; he merely stared back through his narrow slits.

"Come now, it was you following both Watson and Stephan from the pub that night, your large frame makes identification unmistakable."

The Okhrana agent icily said, "I am not one of your English policemen. My target was Stephan. If you had not interfered, this plot might already be extinguished."

Holmes grunted. "Yes I suppose another *accident* might have occurred." My colleague stood and retrieved his pipe from the mantel. "These men have proved devious, cunning, resourceful and able. I find it hard to imagine that they have not worked out a method for getting at these ministers. If you do not mind, I would like to be left to consider the problem," he said, pulling a pinch of tobacco from the slipper. "Mr. Downing, call again tomorrow morning and we will discuss the matter further."

CHAPTER 9

Next morning I awoke to solitude. Once again Holmes had risen before me and vacated Baker Street. A note sat in the middle of the table. The missive gave no indication as to where he had gone, or what his errand might be, but it instructed that I contact Mr. Downing at the Foreign Office and request he return to Baker Street at noon.

"Holmes! Where have you been?" I asked impatiently as my friend burst into the room shortly after eleven o'clock.

"You contacted Downing?" he questioned, ignoring my query.

"Yes, he should keep the appointment. But where have you been?" I repeated.

Holmes took a seat and waved me toward the sofa opposite him.

"I have located their workshop."

"You have?" I bellowed. "How?"

My friend lit his pipe. "Last night as I pondered the problem, I thought back to our interview with Mr. Kropetsky. Do you recall when he became ever so slightly animated, commending us for opposing the Tsar in the Crimean War?"

"Yes," I replied, remembering that it was the one instance when the scientist's suave demeanor had broken.

"During that interlude, he chastised that Britain was presently engaged in military cooperation with Imperial Russia against the Boxers in China and also said *that our government was even speaking of a new economic agreement with the Tsar.* Downing stated that the arrival of the Tsar's ministers and the content of their mission is a closely guarded secret. Mr. Kropetsky betrayed knowledge he should not have possessed."

"So he *is* in league with the conspirators?" I gasped.

"I thought it unlikely, Watson, but I knew that he had been selective in the information he had provided us. I believed that he was playing both sides in an attempt to keep good faith with his left-wing brethren while currying enough favor with we Britons to ensure that he would not be exiled from our country. I took the earliest train to Harrow and I put it to him straight. He was as crafty as ever and I must admit that I had to resort to a rather unsavory tactic in order to pry more material from him."

Holmes drew heartily on his pipe before continuing. "Without revealing the true situation, I explained that the state of affairs was dire and that if he did not furnish me more information, I would implicate him in the matter and that he could expect a visit from Mr. Sharpoff before the day was out."

"You threatened to incriminate him even though you believed he was not a party to the scheme?" said I with a tone of admonishment.

Holmes sighed. "Yes. As I said, I had to resort to an unsavory method. Although I must admit it troubles me very little, Watson. Mr. Kopertsky's halfway measures were selfishly meant to aid only himself rather than benefit either us, *or* his radical friends."

"Obviously, your maneuver had the desired effect," I returned, thinking of Kropetsky's aversion to an encounter with the brutish Okhrana agent.

"He was still guarded, but the threat did get him moving. He assured me that he did not know of the anarchists' dealings first hand but that he could likely attain some information through an acquaintance and asked that he be allowed to keep his source confidential. I told him that I would allow it, but that if he held back from me, I would still turn Sharpoff loose on him. He scribbled a note and had a lad hurry off with it. Before long a reply came with the address of an abandoned machine shop. He swore that he could provide nothing more."

"Do you believe him?" I asked.

A cloud of blue smoke obscured my friend's face for an instant. "I am certain that *he* has no more information. However if things go awry we may have to squeeze the name of his source from him. He implored me not to pursue such a tact and I assured him I would not unless I was forced by circumstances to do so."

"Do you have any suspicions as to this source?"

"Oh, I am certain that it is one of his fellow exiles, perhaps one who although not part of the plot is a bit more sincere in his beliefs

114

than our scientist friend and may have provided some funds or helped the conspirators find lodgings. The members of this gang are after all strangers to London."

I stood and began walking toward my bedroom to retrieve my revolver. "Should we collect Gregson before heading to their workshop?" I asked over my shoulder.

"There is no need. I have already been there. They are gone."

"Gone?" I asked, turning back toward him in disbelief. "Then what good did Kropetsky's information do?"

"Their bags are there, packed. They will return to collect them. But not before they make their attempt. I thought through this little problem last night, Watson and it seems most probable that they will strike at the site of the meetings. If they use their device to destroy the building as the negotiations are taking place they will not only murder the Tsar's officials, but our own as well, which will eliminate the most qualified men from both governments. It is unlikely that suitable replacements could be found before the western money markets contract, as Mr. Downing said is predicted to occur."

"I hope that Mr. Tesla can construct his counter-device in time," said I with a hint of desperation in my voice.

"I have been to see him as well," Holmes stated. "He is finishing the machine as we speak and should have it ready within the hour."

Mr. Downing arrived at the prescribed time, but the dour Okhrana agent was not with him.

"Where is your Russian friend?" Holmes asked.

"He is keeping an eye on the delegation," replied Downing.

Without mention of Mr. Kropetsky, Holmes informed that he believed the attempt would be made upon the site of the meetings.

"My heavens!" the Foreign Office official blurted, consulting his pocket-watch, "The first round of discussions is to be held in just an hour!"

"Let us make haste then!" Holmes said brightly; almost jovial at the prospect of a showdown with the plotters. "At what address?"

Downing named a building near Whitehall, not far from the Foreign Office. Since the meetings were to be clandestine, it was thought imprudent to conduct the negotiations at the main building where their arrival might be observed by the press.

"Very good," said Holmes. "Oh we have set a nice little trap for them," my friend chortled with delight, rubbing his hands together. "Watson, do collect your service revolver and head off with Mr. Downing. I will stop for Mr. Tesla and meet you. Station yourself across the street, in some inconspicuous position. We do not want to scare them off," said he, dropping his hat upon his head and reaching for his walking stick.

As Mr. Downing and I left our rooms I handed Billy a message to be delivered to Gregson. In it I gave a brief account of Holmes's conclusions and asked that he meet us at the site of the negotiations. I warned that if he were to bring officers, they should be few in number and in plain clothes as we did not want to tip our hand and ruin our ambush.

The building was of brown stone, five stories in height. The first floor had no windows, although shallow arched alcoves occupied the spaces where windows might have been. A structure where government business might be conducted could be expected to be devoid of windows on the first floor, but I expect that this design was for architectural aesthetics, and it gave a pleasing, almost Romanesque look to an otherwise drab utilitarian English edifice.

The street was busy as throngs of pedestrians lined the avenue and cabs, wagons, carts and vans of all shapes and sizes formed an endless procession in both directions. Although the building and its neighbors were nowhere near as impressive as the stately grandeur of Whitehall, a great deal of government business was conducted in the block as these outliers served as annexes to numerous cabinet departments. Therefore Mr. Downing, with his dapper dress and proper grooming did not appear out of place in the active crowd teeming throughout the area.

"In here," I said, pulling the Foreign Office representative into the vestibule of a building across the street. We had not been in the spot two minutes when Holmes appeared at my elbow.

"Watson," he said in a low voice. "This way." Mr. Downing and I followed Holmes around the corner to a cramped alleyway.

My friend pushed open a narrow wooden door that closed the passageway off from the street. Packed in the constricted little alley we found Inspectors Gregson and Lestrade as well as Mr. Tesla.

"Gentlemen," said Holmes. "We have laid a splendid little snare for this wicked lot. Watson and I can identify both Stephan and this mismatched eyed fellow called 'Dimitri.' Watson, you Lestrade and Mr. Downing are to stay in that spot you so aptly picked across the street from the meeting place. If you spy the pair, corral them. Lestrade has his whistle and he and Gregson informed me that there are a number of plain clothed officers milling about the street that will rush to your aid. If however, you only mark one of the men, try your best to keep him under surveillance and only move on him if absolutely necessary. If we do not apprehend both of them we will be giving their scheme a life preserver."

Holmes continued, "Mr. Tesla, Gregson and I are going to station ourselves in the rear of the building. There is an alley there that will suit our purpose so as to ensure that the villains do not apply their infernal device from that quarter. If we need assistance, Gregson and I both have a whistle. If you hear it, come our way. If they somehow employ the device before either of our teams apprehends them..." he tapped a small leather bag carried by Tesla. "We will make saving the delegation a priority." My colleague then slipped from the passage, followed by Gregson and the inventor.

"Gentlemen," said I. "Shall we be off?"

"Lead the way, Doctor," replied Lestrade, a grimace upon his ferret-like face.

We had been at our post no more than a quarter of an hour when Downing hissed, "There they are!"

Startled, Lestrade and I both moved forward. Suddenly I recalled that Downing did not know the plotters by sight and the true nature of his exclamation revealed itself when I spotted the large figure of Sharpoff leading three well-dressed men into the building. A second man, whom I presumed to be Sharpoff's Okhrana counterpart, brought up the rear.

I put a restraining hand on Lestrade's arm. "It is the delegation." I felt the inspector's muscles relax as he pulled back into the vestibule.

An hour passed and despite a constant vigil I did not see either of the conspirators. I must admit that it was an anxiety-ridden ordeal trying to scan every face in the ever-changing flow of urbanites. Another hour elapsed and perspiration dripped from beneath my bowler. It was not a particularly hot day, but the stress of attempting to scrutinize every face that came by was taking its toll upon me. As the minute-hand made its third lap of the dial I finally spied a familiar face. However, it was not one of the conspirators. The narrow-eyed Sharpoff stepped from the building followed by his three charges and lastly his partner. He funneled the ministers down the street and they disappeared from view.

"I thought Mr. Holmes said that they would strike here?" Downing said as he nervously mopped his brow with his handkerchief.

"Sir, if you don't mind, could you run around behind the building and tell Mr. Holmes that the ministers have left?" I said to Downing.

"Yes, certainly," he replied, stepping from the foyer.

"I had my doubts, Doctor," Lestrade stated. "I'll grant you that the chap by the rail station was a member of some group of Russian malcontents but I'm still confident that his death was simply the result of a drunken accident. I don't doubt there are radicals in the city but it seems that their presence has caused Mr. Holmes's imagination to run away from him. I mean, you must admit this machine seems a bit far-fetched. Have you even seen a demonstration of it? Even on a small scale?"

I had to admit that I had not. "However, Mr. Tesla is perhaps the most highly regarded man in his field. If he says…" I was cut off as Holmes, Tesla, and Gregson appeared. Lestrade and I stepped from our hiding place and we formed a small congregation upon the pavement. A few seconds later, Mr. Downing came rushing across the street, having just exited the building where the meetings had occurred.

Holmes looked troubled. His brows were knitted and he stared at the ground, his chin resting in his hand.

"They have adjourned for the day," Downing said as he joined our group.

"That must be it," Holmes stated, his thoughts resulting in some private conclusion. Looking up he said, "The rascals ran into some impediment; perhaps an issue with their machine. Negotiations of this type are never concluded in one session. They will make their attempt when the meetings renew."

"They will not return today," Downing interjected. "They are attending a reception at the ambassador's residence.

"Is it close by?" I asked, remembering that the delegation did not board a coach.

"Why yes, not two blocks."

"I am sorry for creating such haste," Holmes said to the whole gathering. "However, we needed to be ready to spring our trap as soon as the negotiations began. There was no way to know that they would not strike today. Will the ministers meet at the same time tomorrow?" Holmes asked Downing.

"That is their intention."

"Thank you gentlemen," said Holmes to the assemblage. "We shall meet back here tomorrow..." he said, consulting his watch, "...at half twelve."

Lestrade and Gregson left together, the former grumbling his discontent over the situation while the latter politely tried to defend the conclusions that he shared with Sherlock Holmes.

Downing, Tesla, Holmes and I lingered for a few minutes, speculating over how many days the negotiations might last and the likelihood that the attack would come upon the morrow.

"Although discussions of this sort normally take time, the matter could conceivably be concluded in a relatively short duration," Downing said.

"Yes," added Holmes. "That is why we needed to be on the ready and must assume that had it been possible they would have struck today. Unless they again encounter some extreme difficulty it seems tomorrow will be----."

The final words of my friend's sentence were obscured as a large wagon drawn by four horses thundered past. As the wagon continued by, my companion's features contorted into the most bizarre expression. First shock, then alarm consumed his visage. Suddenly I noticed that despite the departure of the wagon, the rumble remained and I felt a slight vibration under my feet.

"The reception!" Holmes exclaimed. "The ambassador's home! The address!" he cried, grabbing Downing by the shoulders. "What is the address?"

A look of fright descended upon Mr. Downing's face and he began to stammer, finally belching out the street and number after what felt like eons. Upon the information reaching his ears, Holmes grabbed hold of his hat and took off at sprint.

"This way," I exclaimed to Tesla, tugging at his arm. The two of us hustled off after Holmes, and Mr. Downing fell in behind us.

As I ran, I felt the street trembling beneath my footfalls. At first it was a subtle feeling, I dare say no more than a buzz. However as we drew closer to the Russian ambassador's residence, the vibrations, and the drone that accompanied them increased. Not only did the pulsations grow as we neared the epicenter, so did the reaction of the pedestrians. When we first took off after Holmes, the sensation seemed to go largely unnoticed by the preoccupied city-dwellers but the nearer we got to the site of the attack, the greater the confusion in the streets.

It was no more than two minutes before we reached our destination. The building was three stories in height and made of smoke-gray brick. The first and second floor windows were caged with iron bars and although the measure was surely meant as security for the Russian ambassador, our adversaries had deviously inverted their purpose: now the bars would keep the men imprisoned, unable to leap to safety. I stood in awestruck wonderment as the structure shook. The movement was slight, but increasing in intensity with each passing moment.

Confused and panicky pedestrians cast bizarre looks at the building as they scurried away in all directions. A horse reared in front of us, threatening to upset the cart it pulled. I jumped toward the animal and caught hold of its bridle, ordering the driver to climb down and lead the animal away with all possible haste. Just as the wagon passed us, Holmes came running into view from around the side of the building.

"They have padlocked the doors. Both front and back!" he stated. "I could not find their device on the outside. It must be affixed within. Mr. Tesla, where should you apply your apparatus?" asked Holmes.

The Serbian genius ran over to the building and put both of his palms against the vibrating wall. "This corner!" he spat out, pointing toward the far left of the structure. "Their machine must be somewhere near the back, opposite this corner. To most efficiently counter its effects this would be the most opportune spot," said he as he pulled a breadbox sized gadget from the leather bag.

Tesla pushed the machine up against the corner. Each side of the instrument was fitted with a handle that turned a thick screw. As the handles were spun, the screws would extend, clamping the device to the building. The engineer's deft fingers worked furiously, trying to lengthen the screws evenly, but the ever increasing movement of the stone wall made his job extremely difficult. Suddenly, I heard a "ping" and a coin-sized fragment of the building chipped off just above Tesla's head.

Holmes instantly grabbed the scientist and pulled him around the corner of the doomed structure. "Watson! Get Downing!" he yelled as he disappeared. Instantly I realized the danger and dragged the diplomat into the alley.

"Where is he?" I asked desperately.

"Where is who?" Downing broke in, a confused panic coating his voice.

"There is a sniper!" I hissed at him, turning back to Holmes.

"Atop that building," Holmes pointed across the street with his cane as a drizzle of dislodged mortar from the vibrating building rained down upon us. "Gentlemen, Watson and I will try to dispense with that rifleman. I still have my police whistle. If you hear it, you will be clear to affix the machine. If however the sound does not reach your ears before you deem it unsafe to remain near this building; by all means depart."

I felt a shove to my shoulder and thought that it had been my friend, urging me forward. However, I was mistaken. The building itself had knocked into me.

"This way Watson," said Holmes, beckoning me to follow him down the alley toward the rear of the building.

We hustled through the passageway and were just turning to make our way behind the adjacent building when my arm was caught in a vice-like grip. "And where are you going?" an icy Russian accent asked.

CHAPTER 10

"Mr. Sharpoff," I gasped. "I thought you were trapped within!"

"Almost," he uttered. "I stepped out to get some tobacco. Where are you going?" he grumbled emotionlessly.

"Mr. Tesla cannot apply his counter-device as there is a sniper on the rooftop across the street. We are on our way to deal with him."

"Sharpoff," Holmes barked. "Time is of the essence. Come or stay. It is up to you." With that my friend hurried onward. The Okhrana agent grimaced at the chastisement but did not reply, choosing to fall in behind us.

We emerged on the nearest cross street where the panicked bewilderment as to what might actually be occurring had resulted in many men and women taking flight away from the ambassador's house while others simply stared in mystification at the quivering building.

Holmes raced across the street and pushed his back to a storefront. Sharpoff and I mimicked my friend and our procession quickly skirted the buildings until we had reached the one my colleague had determined housed the anarchist marksman. It was an office building and as we entered, we had to squeeze by the employees as they vacated in a mixture of fear and perplexed curiosity at the happenings just across the avenue.

My friend ran quickly up the stairwell and at the fifth floor, he raced to the rear of the building where after a quick examination he found a portal leading to the stairs that reached the roof. We likewise ascended this set of stairs where a small shack-like structure housed the door that opened out to the roof.

"Mr. Sharpoff, are you armed?"

"Da," the Tsar's enforcer replied, pulling a smart looking pistol from his coat.

Holmes withdrew his own revolver and motioned that I do likewise. The prospect of surprising an armed assailant is one that any prudent individual would only undertake with a stealthy caution. Unfortunately, time was of the essence. Each passing moment brought us closer to the collapse of the ambassador's home, and the likely death of all within. Therefore I could not argue with the audacity of Holmes's plan.

"Gentlemen, if my calculations are correct, the sniper is straight ahead of this door; approximately fifty feet or so. We will burst out as quickly as possible and take refuge behind this shed," said he, knocking on the wall. "Shoot to kill," Holmes added in a dark tone. "Ready? Now!"

As the door exploded forward I caught a glimpse of the mismatched eyed Dimitri at the edge of the rooftop holding a carbine. His shocked expression lasted a split second as he suddenly spun his rifle toward us. However the sniper was not alone. Beside him knelt the bearded Stephan, who drew a pistol from his waistband and leveled it in our direction.

We three all found asylum behind the shack, and not a moment too soon as the sound of bullets riddled the structure. Holmes, Sharpoff and I all returned fire. There was no precision in our aim as we poked around the corner of the shed, squeezing off rounds. Abruptly, there was silence.

Holmes laid himself flat upon the ground and sneaked his head around the edge of the shack. He sat up quickly and pulled the whistle from his breast pocket and blew several shrill notes.

"The rifle is abandoned," he said, opening the chamber of his revolver. "I am out," he announced with some disgust.

"As am I," said I after examining my own gun.

The Russian made no comment. Either he did not understand our meaning or did not care to enlighten us as to his status.

Standing, Holmes led the way warily around the shack. "Be careful. Stephan is still armed, and Dimitri may have a pistol as well."

As we cleared the shed, I heard Holmes call out, "There!" I followed the walking stick with which my friend pointed, to see the tall form of Dimitri leaping to the next building.

"And there!" I added, as I spied Stephan in the opposite direction. He was already climbing down a metal ladder two buildings away.

"I will go after Dimitri," Sharpoff croaked as he began to run.

"This way, Watson!" Holmes clapped a hand on my shoulder and we hurried after the other anarchist.

We ran across the second building and peered downward to make sure the rogue was not laying in wait. However, there was no sign of him and we quickly descended the iron rungs.

"Do you feel that, Watson?" Holmes asked as I dropped next to him.

I smiled broadly. "The ground is not moving! Tesla has done it!"

"We still have time to net that scoundrel Stephan. I am sure he is headed to collect his things at their workshop. Let's be off!" my friend said, hailing a cab as we stepped from the alleyway into the street.

In no more than twenty minutes we climbed from the hansom a block from the abandoned machine shop that had functioned as the conspirator's work place. Holmes led the way behind the building to a boarded up window.

"Do you believe that he has beaten us here?" I asked.

Holmes pushed at one of the wide planks blocking the opening and it slid neatly to one side. He put his nose close to the sill, examining the dust.

"He is inside," Holmes whispered. My friend peered through the opening, surveying what he could of the interior. He became thoughtful for a moment. "He will be wary coming out of this window. I do not think we could surprise him here and you and I are both without ammunition. We must go in."

Holmes slid through the opening and I quietly followed. I nearly upset an old, grimy, still filled water cooler as I entered the dim room. Inside was a large space littered with work tables, and several dozen bulky machines, some of which were covered with drop cloths. We could hear movement at the far end of the room, although that distant corner was too far away to see from our vantage point.

"Watson, he has his revolver, but we also know that this man is skilled with a knife," Holmes whispered close to my ear. "However, he does not know that our guns are empty. I want you to head back to where he is, as stealthily as possible. Approach slowly and carefully; be sure not to announce yourself. I will join you presently. We shall try to bluff him into surrendering."

"And if he does not surrender?"

Holmes smiled and patted me on the back. "Off you go, Watson."

I did not relish the idea of confronting the man. He was still armed and at this point, terribly desperate. However, I trusted Holmes's judgment in such matters and if he felt that this was the best course of action, there could be no doubting that it was. I crept as silently as I could, using the ghostly shapes of the covered machines to blind my approach. After an agonizing five minutes, I reached the far corner and peering over a shrouded contraption.

Holmes pushed at one of the wide planks blocking the opening and it slid neatly to one side.

131

There stood the anarchist with his back to me. He was burning a pile of papers in a tin wastebasket. The flames leaped and then died. Stephan peered into the can and apparently contented, grabbed the handle of the satchel that rested on a cot. At that moment Holmes appeared beside me.

"Stephan!" he called out. "Do not move! You are under arrest!"

The would-be assassin raised his pistol, scanning the darkness with narrowed eyes.

"We are here, Stephan," Holmes said loudly. "It is Dr. Watson and I, Sherlock Holmes. Kindly drop your weapon and surrender yourself."

My jaw dropped in abject shock as my friend not only exposed our location, but illuminated the villain to the fact that we were alone. The Russian however did not fire upon us, nor assault our position. Rather, he took off at a dead run along the far wall. I took a step to follow but Holmes's hand restrained me.

"Not yet."

A moment later an anguished scream pierced the air and then silence.

"Come, Watson," he said. Holmes led the way back toward the window we had used to enter the building. There lying in a pool of water was the limp form of the Russian revolutionary.

"But what happened?" I said, stepping closer.

"Hold there, Watson," said Holmes, blocking my way with his cane. He inched closer, careful not to step in the puddle. He

132

reached out his walking stick and used it to lift a pair of copper wires from the liquid and tossed them ten feet away onto the bare cement floor. "Now Watson, see if he lives. But be cautious that he is not trying to dupe us; remember the knife that nearly did you in once before."

I rushed to the man's side and felt for a pulse. "He is dead, Holmes."

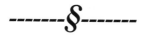

I leaned back in the comfortable chair in our sitting room. "So you wired a series of batteries together, poured the water from the cooler upon the floor, and then dropped the leads into the pool of water? A neat trap, Holmes."

"My dear Watson, I told you that I learned of Mr. Tesla while educating myself regarding a case where electricity was used as the means to commit murder. I merely replicated the method employed in that crime. I noticed the dry cells upon my first visit to the place, although I must admit, at that time I had no hint that they might play a part."

"And I presume that your 'bluff' was to make Stephan take flight toward your trap."

"I was certain that he would never actually surrender, so by announcing that you and I were the only pursuers on the premises,

133

Stephan believed he had a clear egress through the window to freedom. Ah, here comes Downing and Sharpoff is with him," Holmes said, pushing the curtains to one side.

The men were shown in by Billy and the Foreign Office man did not even wait to remove his hat before striding across to where we stood. He gave each of our hands a vigorous shake. "Thank you, gentlemen! Thank you. You have done two countries a tremendous service."

"Do sit down," Holmes instructed. "Mrs. Hudson should be delivering tea any moment; ah here she is! Thank you Mrs. Hudson," he said as she deposited the service upon the table and efficiently poured us each a cup.

"You're very welcome, gentlemen. Enjoy," our noble landlady called as she scurried out through the door.

"No tea, Mr. Sharpoff?" Holmes smiled as the stoic Russian waved off the cup I tried to hand him. "Oh well I suppose without the lemon it is not to your liking."

Mr. Downing readily accepted his tea however, taking the seat next to the Tsar's man.

"If you do not mind," Holmes said, taking a sip from his cup. "I should like to inquire about the other villain in this little play. Mr. Sharpoff, did you capture Dimitri?"

"He fell to the street trying to escape," the tight-lipped Russian answered, stone faced.

A wry smile flitted across Holmes's lips. "Yes, I suppose it was another case of death by misadventure."

Sensing our mistrust, Mr. Downing quickly tried to change the subject. "Mr. Telsa's counter-measure device was a complete success. The ministers are alive and well. Once the immediate threat had been neutralized, we had the padlocks cut away and smashed their machine to bits. It was in the basement, you know."

Downing continued, "And Mr. Tesla has graciously agreed to distribute the plans for his defensive machine to any and all governments who wish it. In the future, if there are any who hope to employ an oscillation device as a weapon, they will be disappointed," he smiled.

The pair stayed for a half hour and even though the danger seemed to have evaporated, both men still had obligations to the diplomatic envoys they served and thus needed to be on their way. The Russian left with nothing more than a slight bow which contrasted greatly with the effusive thanks issued by Mr. Downing.

"So Holmes," I said handing my friend a cigar. "We began by investigating the curious death of that Boris chap by the rail station and in trying to bring justice for the murdered man we ended by thwarting the very plot to which he was a party."

Holmes laughed. "Poetic is it not? I should think that would appeal to your nature, Watson. After all it is your penchant for highlighting such romantic novelties in the little sketches you write up."

135

"I suppose that Mr. Kropetsky can resume his role as society darling and radical journalist."

Holmes shrugged. "If his fellow agitators do not realize the aide he had given us and mark him as a traitor. As I said before Watson, he walks a precarious line trying to reap the benefits of celebrity while bemoaning the 'oppression' of the working class."

I frowned. "It is too bad that Gregson was not present as we tied up the loose ends with Downing and Sharpoff."

"Quite," Holmes returned. "Do be a good fellow and drop by the Yard to fill him in when you have the opportunity. Now if you do not mind, hand me that *Times*. I should like to examine today's agony column."

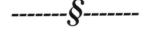

Made in the USA
Lexington, KY
06 September 2015